THE TYCOON'S
RELUCTANT
CINDERELLA

THE TYCOON'S RELUCTANT CINDERELLA

BY

THERESE BEHARRIE

MILLS & BOON

First published in Great Britain 2016
By Mills & Boon, an imprint of HarperCollins*Publishers*
1 London Bridge Street, London, SE1 9GF

Large Print edition 2017

© 2016 Therese Beharrie

ISBN: 978-0-263-07097-2

Printed and bound in Great Britain
by CPI Antony Rowe, Chippenham, Wiltshire

This book is dedicated to my husband,
my best friend and my biggest supporter,

Grant, thank you for working so hard so that
I could follow my dream. Thank you for
believing that I would be a published author
when writing was only a vague possibility
for my future. And, most of all, thank you for
loving me so well that there is
no doubt in my mind that good men
and happily-ever-afters exist. I love you.

To my family and friends,

Thank you all for supporting me.
For listening to me as I went on about my
dream of writing and the plans I had to get
published. To those who allowed me to talk
about plot lines and characters even though
it might have bored you, thank you.
You have all contributed to this,
and I am so grateful.

To my editor,

Flo, you invested time and effort in me
even though there was no guarantee I would
be worth it. Over and above that, I have
experienced so much growth as a writer
in the months we've worked together.
I can't wait to continue this journey with you.
Thank you for everything.

CHAPTER ONE

'PLEASE HOLD THE ELEVATOR!'

Callie McKenzie almost shouted the words as she ran to the closing doors. She was horribly late, despite her rushed efforts to get dressed after her shift at the hotel had ended. She wouldn't be making a very good impression on the big boss if she arrived after he did, so she was taking a chance on the elevator, ignoring her usual reservations about the small box.

Relief shot through her when she saw a hand hold the elevator doors and she hurried in, almost colliding with the person who had helped her. She had meant to say thank you immediately, but as she looked at him her mouth dried, taking her words away.

Callie thought he might be the most beautiful man she had ever seen. Dark hair sat tousled on his head, as though it had travelled through whirlwinds to get there, and set off the sea-blue-green of his eyes. He was a full head taller than her, so that she had to look up to appreciate the striking features of his face. Each angle was shaped perfectly—as though it had been sculpted, she thought, with the intention of causing every woman who looked at it to be caught in involuntary—or voluntary—attraction.

Her eyes fell to his lips as they curved into a smile and she felt her heart flutter. It was the kind of smile that transformed his entire face, giving it a sexy, casual expression that stood out against the sophistication of his perfectly tailored suit. It took her a while to realise that she was amusing him by staring, and she forced herself to snap out of it.

'Thank you,' she said, aware of the husky undertone her evaluation of him had brought to her voice.

His smile broadened. 'No problem. Which floor would you like?'

Callie almost slapped her hand against her forehead at the deep baritone of his voice. Was there *anything* about the man that wasn't sexy?

She cleared her throat. 'Ground floor, please.'

'Then it's already been selected,' he said, and

pressed the button to close the elevator doors. 'So you're also going to the event downstairs, then?'

She frowned. 'Yes. How did you know?'

'Well, I'd like to think that this hotel doesn't require its guests to dress up in such formal wear to have supper.'

He gestured to her clothing, and Callie once again resisted the urge to slap herself on the head. She was wearing one of her mother's formal gowns—one of the few Callie *didn't* think was absolutely ridiculous—and nodded.

'Of course. Sorry, it's been a long day.' Callie wished she believed that was the reason for her lame responses, but she knew better. She wasn't sure why, but he threw her off balance.

'I can relate. This isn't the most ideal way to spend the evening.'

Callie was about to agree when the elevator came to an abrupt stop. The lights went out barely a second later and Callie lost her balance, knocking her head into the back wall. The world spun for a bit, and then she felt strong arms hold her and lower her to the ground.

'Are you okay?' he asked, and Callie had to

take a moment to catch her breath before she answered.

She wasn't sure if she was dizzy because she was in his arms or because of the blow to her head. Or, she thought as the situation finally caught up to her, if it was her very real fear of being trapped in enclosed spaces that had affected her breathing.

'I'm fine.' Her breath hitched, but she forced it out slowly. 'I'm sure it's just a bump on the head.' *Inhale, exhale,* she reminded herself.

'Are you sure? You're breathing quite heavily.'

Her eyes had now acclimatised to the darkness, and she could see the concern etched on his face. 'I'm a little…claustrophobic.'

'Ah.' He nodded his head and stood. 'The electricity must have gone off, but I'm sure it won't take long before someone realises we're here.'

He removed his phone from his pocket and tapped against the screen. A light shone dimly between them but Callie could only see his face, disproportionately large in the poor light. She felt a strange mixture of disappointment and satisfaction that she couldn't make out his features as clearly as she had before, but she did manage to make out the scowl on his face.

'I don't have any reception, so I can't call anyone to help.'

'You could press that button over there,' she said helpfully, pointing to the red emergency button on the control panel.

Her breathing was coming a little easier—as long as she didn't think about the fact that she was trapped. She wanted to stand up, but didn't trust herself to be steady. And the last thing she wanted was to fall into the arms of her companion for a second time within a few minutes.

'Of course I can.'

He pressed the emergency button and quickly conversed with the static voice that came through the intercom. He'd been right. There had been a power outage in the entire grid, and the hotel's generator had for some reason gone off as well. They were assured that it was being sorted out, but that it might take up to thirty minutes before they would be rescued.

He sighed and sank down next to her, and Callie squeezed her eyes shut. She thought it might make his proximity—and her fear—less overwhelming. Instead, the smell of him filled her senses—a musky male scent that almost made her sigh in satisfaction. She swore she could hear her heart throbbing in her chest, but she told herself it was just because of the confines of the elevator. She opened her eyes and looked at him, and before she could become mesmerised by his looks—even in the dim light he was handsome— forced herself to speak.

'I wonder what's going on downstairs. There must be mass panic.' She couldn't quite keep the scorn from colouring her voice.

'I take it that you're not a fan of tonight's celebrations,' he said wryly.

'I wouldn't say that. I'm just…' she searched for the word '…sceptical.'

'About the event, or the reason for it?'

The innocent question brought a flurry of emotions that she wasn't ready to face. Her brother, Connor, had warned her that the hotel they both worked at hadn't been doing well for years now. Despite his efforts as regional manager, Connor was still struggling to bring the Elegance Hotel back from the mess the last manager had created. The arrival today of the CEO—their boss—held a mass of implications that she didn't want to think about.

So, instead of answering his question, she asked, 'Are you here to meet the CEO?'

'Not really, no.'

'A very cryptic answer.'

She could sense his smile.

'I like the idea of being a little mysterious.'

She laughed. 'You realise I don't know who you are, right? Everything about you is mysterious to me.'

As she said the words she turned towards him and found herself face to face with him. Her heart pounded, her breath slowed, and for the briefest moment she wanted to lean forward and kiss him.

The thought was as effective as ice down her back, and she shifted away, blaming claustrophobia for her physical reaction to a man she barely knew.

She shook her head, and was brought back to the reality of the situation. Soon she didn't have to pretend to blame her shortness of breath on her fear. She felt a hand grip her own and looked at him. She could see the concern in his eyes, and gratitude filled her when she realised that reassurance, not attraction, was the reason for his gesture.

'Your date must be worried about you,' he said, and nodded, encouraging her to concentrate on his words.

'He might be,' she agreed, 'if I had brought one.'

He laughed, and the sound was as manly as the rest of him. What *was* it about the man that enthralled all her senses?

'And yours?' Callie asked, and wondered at herself. This wasn't like her. She was flirting with him. And even though she knew that she shouldn't, she wanted to know the answer.

Their eyes locked, and once again something sizzled between them.

'I don't have a date here.'

'Your girlfriend couldn't make it tonight?'

She turned away from him as she asked the question, and leaned her head back against the elevator wall. She didn't want to succumb to the magnetism that surrounded him, but she had already failed miserably. She shouldn't be asking him about his personal life. But every time she looked at him her heart kicked in her chest and she wanted to know more. If she looked away, the walls began to close in on her.

So she chose the lesser of the two evils and turned back to him. His eyes were patient, steady, and she gave in to the temptation. 'Couldn't she?'

'There's no girlfriend.'

Was she imagining the slight tension in his voice?

'And you don't have a boyfriend, I assume?'

'You assume correctly—although I probably shouldn't be telling you that.'

'Why not?'

'Well, you're a strange man and we're stuck in an elevator together. What's going to deter you from putting the moves on me now that you know I don't have a boyfriend?'

Callie said the words before she could think about what they might provoke. But he just said, 'You don't have to worry about that. I don't "put the moves" on anyone.'

'So women just drop at your feet, then?' She couldn't take her eyes off him as she dug deeper.

'Sometimes.'

He smiled, but even in the dim light she could

see something in his eyes that she couldn't decipher.

'Ah, modesty. Charming.' She said it in jest, but her heart sank. This man—this very attractive man who made her heart beat faster just by looking at her—wasn't interested in *one* woman. *Women* fell at his feet—and she wouldn't be one of them.

He laughed, and then sobered. 'Mostly I stay away from them.'

Callie felt herself soften just a little at the heartbreak she could hear ever so slightly in his voice. And just like that her judgement of him faded away. He didn't want women, or even just one woman—he wanted to be alone. Callie couldn't figure out which fact bothered her the most.

'I'm sorry. She must have been a real piece of work.'

He didn't answer her, but his face told her everything that she needed to know. She placed a hand over his and squeezed it, hoping to provide him with some comfort. But when he laid his hand over hers in return, comfort was the last thing on her mind. His hand brought heat to hers, and lit her heart so that it beat to a rhythm she couldn't fathom. He leaned his head towards hers, and suddenly heat spread through her bloodstream.

This couldn't be right, she thought desperately as she pulled her hand away. They barely knew each other. She wouldn't let herself fall into a web of attraction with a man who was as charming as a fairy-tale prince.

Before she could worry about it the elevator lurched and the lights came back on. He stood and offered a hand to her, a slight smile on his gorgeous face. Did he know the effect he had on her? Or was he simply aware that he'd helped distract her from one of her worst fears?

As Callie took his hand she had to admit that he *had* kept her thoughts off being stuck in an elevator. And she blamed that—and his good looks—on her uncharacteristic reaction.

'Thank you,' she said as the elevator doors opened. 'I hope you enjoy the rest of your evening.'

The breath of relief that was released from her lungs as she walked away was because she was out of the enclosed space, Callie assured herself, and ignored the voice in her head that scoffed at the lie.

* * *

Blake Owen stopped at the doors of the banquet hall and resisted the urge to walk away. He had never been a fan of opulence, but rarely did he have a choice in the matter. Which was fine, he supposed. In his business, events of an extravagant nature were integral to success, and the welcome for him tonight was an excellent example of that. He would be introduced to the Elegance Hotel in Cape Town in a style that would keep the hotel's name at the forefront of the media's attention while he sorted out the troublesome operation.

So he accepted his lot and walked into the room, snagging a flute of champagne from the nearest waiter's tray before taking the whole scene in.

Glamour spread from the roof to the floor and fairy lights and sparkling chandeliers twinkled like stars against the midnight-blue draping. Black-and-white-clad waiters wove through the crowd while men and women in tuxedos and evening gowns air-kissed and wafted around on clouds of self-importance.

Blake almost rolled his eyes—until he remembered the guests were there in *his* honour. The thought made him empty the entire champagne glass and exchange it for a full one from the next waiter. He noted that the power outage hadn't seemed to dampen the evening's festivities. But when he looked at the scene with the eye of a manager he could see some slightly frazzled members of staff weaving through the crowd doing damage control.

He managed to get the attention of one of them, and took the frightened young man to a less populated corner of the hall.

'What happened when the electricity went out?'

As Blake spoke the man's eyes widened and Blake thought that 'boy' might be a more appropriate description.

'It was only a few moments, sir. As you can see, everything is running smoothly again. Enjoy your evening.'

The boy made to move away, but at Blake's look he paused.

'Was there anything else, sir?'

'Yes, actually. I was wondering if you brush off the concerns of *all* your guests, or if you reserve that for just a handful of people.'

If the boy had looked nervous before, he was terrified now. 'No...no, sir. I'm sorry you feel that I did. We're just a bit busy, and I have to make sure that everything is okay before Mr Owen gets here.'

'That would be me.'

The words were said in a low voice, softly, but for their effect they might have been earth-shatteringly loud.

'Mr... Mr Owen?' the boy stammered. 'Sir, I am *so* sorry—'

'It's fine,' Blake said when he saw the boy might have a heart attack from the shock. 'You can answer my original question.' At his blank look, Blake elaborated. 'The power outage...?'

'Oh, yes. Well, it wasn't such a train smash here. The candles gave sufficient light that there wasn't much panic, and Connor—Mr McKenzie, I mean—managed to calm whatever concerns there were.'

Blake was surprised the boy had been able to string enough words together to give him such a thorough explanation.

'And that was it?'

'Yes, sir. The generator was back on in under

thirty minutes, so it wasn't too long. Although I *did* hear there were people trapped in the elevator.'

Blake thought it best not to tell the boy *he* had been one of those who had been trapped. He wasn't sure if he would be able to handle another shock.

'When was the last time the generator was checked?'

'I...I don't know, sir.'

Blake nodded and left it at that, making a mental note to check that out when he officially started on Monday. The list of what he would have to do at the hotel seemed to grow the more time he spent there, and he wasn't having it. Not any more. Somehow the Elegance in Cape Town had flown under his radar for the past few years, while he had focused on his other hotels in South Africa.

And while he focused on rebuilding his self-respect after letting himself be fooled into a relationship that should never have been.

When he had eventually started reviewing the financials he'd realised that although Connor McKenzie *had* pulled the hotel out of the mess that Landon Meyer, the previous regional manager, had made, it wasn't enough. The hotel hadn't made a profit for three years, and he couldn't let that continue.

But that wasn't tonight's problem, Blake thought as he scanned the crowd. He knew it would only take a few minutes before he would be recognised, and then he would have to start doing the rounds as guest of honour. He paused when he saw the woman he had been stuck in the elevator with a few moments ago. She was standing near a table full of champagne, and before Blake knew it he was walking towards her.

As he came closer he saw that his recollection of their time spent in the elevator didn't do justice to what he saw now. He had noticed that she was attractive when she'd walked in, but he had taken care not to stare. And with the darkness that had descended only a few moments later, he hadn't been able to look at her as he was now.

The red dress she wore clung only to her chest and then flowed regally down from her waist to the floor. Her black hair stood out strikingly against the dress, her golden skin amplifying the effect, and for reasons he couldn't quite place his finger on it disconcerted him. Her round face held an innocence he hadn't been privy to in a long time, and her green eyes persuaded him to consider pursuing her.

The thought shocked him, as there was nothing in her expression to prompt it. There was also nothing in his past that encouraged him to trust a woman again. Yet now he felt an intense desire to get to know *this* woman. One he had only just met an hour ago.

'I think that after being stuck in an elevator the least we could do is have a drink together.'

Callie heard the deep voice as she reached for a glass of champagne. Her hand stilled, and then she continued, hoping that her pause wouldn't be noticed.

'I don't know if I'm inclined to agree,' she said and took a sip of her drink. 'I never have drinks with anyone I don't know.'

'Really? But you have nothing against flirting with strangers?' He gave her an amused look, his smile widening when she blushed.

'Must have been a temporary lapse in judgement.'

'How do you date if you don't flirt?'

'I don't.' She sipped her drink.

'Which would explain the lack of a boyfriend.'

Callie aimed a level look at him. 'Yes. And it would also explain why I don't have to deal with conversations like this very often.'

'Touché.' He smiled and lifted his glass to her in a toast.

Her lips almost curved in response, but then she stopped herself. What was she *doing*? A memory flashed into her mind, of him sitting with her in the elevator, patiently talking to her to distract her from her fears. And then she remembered. She was flirting with him because there was something about him that had kept her calm when she should have had a panic attack.

Heaven help her.

'And you've told me everything I need to know about why *you're* single, then?' she asked, and immediately regretted it when his expression dimmed. 'I'm sorry, I didn't mean to upset you.'

'No,' he responded, 'it's fine.' But he changed the topic. 'Since you seem to want to know so much about me, how about you offer me the same courtesy? You can start with your name.'

She smiled. 'Callie.'

She held out her hand, proud that her voice revealed none of the strange feelings he evoked in her. He took it and shook it slowly, making the ordinary task feel like an intimate act, and she shifted as a thrill worked its way up her spine.

'Blake? I'm so glad I've found you. I was about to send out a search party.'

Callie stared dumbly at her brother as he strode towards them, his tuxedo perfectly fitted to his build and perfectly suited to his handsome features.

'Hey, Cals, I'm happy you made it without missing too much.' Connor gave her a kiss on the cheek, and angled his face so that Blake wouldn't see his questioning look. 'I see you've met the reason we're all here.'

It took a full minute before Callie could process his words. '*This* is Blake Owen?'

'Yes.' Blake intercepted Connor's reply. 'Although, to be fair, I was about to introduce myself. Connor just got here before I could.'

Blake shook Connor's hand in greeting, and Callie couldn't help but notice how much more efficient the action was now than when he had done it with her.

'How do you two know each other?'

'Connor is my brother,' Callie said, before her brother could say anything. All the feelings inside her had frozen, and she resisted the urge to shiver.

'So you're here to support him? That's great.' Blake smiled at her.

Connor laughed. 'No! Callie's a good sister, but I'm not sure she would attend an event so far out of her comfort zone for *me*.' At Blake's questioning look, Connor elaborated. 'Callie works at the hotel.'

Connor's simple words shattered the opportunity for any explanation Callie might have wanted to give. Blake's eyes iced, and this time she couldn't resist the shiver that went through her body.

'Well, we should probably get going,' Connor said when the silence extended a second too long.

'Yes,' Blake agreed, his gaze never leaving Callie's. 'You should probably start introducing me to the other *employees*—' he said the word with a contempt that Callie hadn't expected '—before I make a mistake I can't rectify.'

Callie watched helplessly as they walked away, wondering how she had already managed to alienate her CEO.

CHAPTER TWO

BLAKE WATCHED AS the crowd in the banquet hall began to thin. There must have been about three hundred people there, he thought. And, the way he felt, he was sure he had spoken to every single one of them. No, he corrected himself almost immediately. Not *everyone*. There was one person he had avoided ever since learning who she was—an employee of the hotel.

Julia, his ex, had been an employee. She had been a part of the Human Resources team in the Port Elizabeth hotel, where he spent most of his time.

He had been enamoured of her. She was beautiful, intelligent, and just a little arrogant. And she had a son who had crept into his heart the moment Blake had met him. It had been a fascinating combination—the gorgeous, sassy woman and the sweet, shy child. One that had lured him in and blinded him to the truth of what she'd wanted from him. The truth that had made him distrust his judgement and conclude that staying away from his employees would be the safest option to avoid getting hurt.

He narrowed his eyes when he saw Callie walking towards him, and cursed himself for the attraction that flashed through his body. But he refused to give in to it. He would ignore the way some strands of her hair had escaped from her hairstyle and floated down to frame her face. He wouldn't notice that she walked as if someone had rolled out a red carpet for her. He hardened himself against the effect she had on him—and then she was in front of him and her smell nearly did him in.

The floral scent was edged with seduction—a description that came from nowhere as she stood innocently in front of him, those emerald eyes clear of any sign of wrongdoing.

'What do you want?' he snapped, and surprised himself. Regardless of the way his body reacted to her, he could control it. He *would* control it.

Her eyes widened, but then set with determination. 'I wanted to set the record straight. I know you must be confused after finding out I work here.'

'That isn't the word I'd use.'

'Well, however you would describe it, I still want to tell you what happened.'

She took a breath, and Blake wondered if she realised how shakily she'd done it.

'I had no idea who you were when we were stuck in that elevator. If I had, I wouldn't have—'

'Flirted with me?'

Something in her eyes fired, and reminded him that he had flirted with her, too. But her voice was calm when she spoke.

'Yes, I suppose. It was an honest mistake. I didn't seek you out to try and soften you up, or anything crazy like that. So...' She paused, and then pushed on. 'Please don't take this out on Connor.'

Blake frowned. She was explaining to him that she'd made a mistake—and the honesty already baffled him—but she didn't seem to be doing it for herself. She was doing it for her brother, and that was...selfless.

Almost everything Julia had done had been self-serving. But then he hadn't known that in the beginning. He'd thought that she was being unselfish, that she was being honest. And those qualities had attracted him. But it had all been pretence. So what if there didn't *seem* to be a deceitful motive behind what Callie was saying? He knew better than anyone else that she might be faking it.

But when he looked at her, into those alluring and devastatingly honest eyes, that thought just didn't sit right.

'So,' he said, sliding his hands into his pockets, 'I can take it out on *you*?'

Was he still flirting with her? No, he thought. He wanted to know what she thought he should do about the situation. Yes, that was it—just a test. How would she respond now that she knew he was her boss?

She cleared her throat. 'If need be, yes. I understand if you feel you need to take disciplinary action, although I don't believe it's necessary.'

'You don't?'

'No, sir.'

The word sounded different coming from her, and he wasn't sure that he liked the way she was defining their relationship.

'I apologise for my unprofessional behaviour, but I assure you it won't happen again.' She looked at him, and this time her eyes pleaded for herself. 'I didn't know who you were. Please give me a chance to make this right.'

Blake was big enough a man to realise when he had made a mistake, and the sincerity the woman in front of him exuded told him he had done just that, in spite of his doubts. He straightened, and saw that there was almost no one left in the room for him to meet. Relief poured through him, and finally he gave himself permission to leave.

But before he did, he said, 'Okay, Miss McKenzie. I believe you. I'll see you at work on Monday.'

By eleven o'clock on Monday morning Blake had had enough. He had got in to the office at six and had been poring over the financials since then. *Again.* But no matter how he looked at it—just as he'd feared the first time he'd reviewed them—there was no denying the fact that this hotel was in serious trouble.

How had he let it get this far? he thought, and walked to the coffee machine in the office he would be sharing with Connor. The man had set up a makeshift space for Blake, which made the place snug, but not unworkable. Right now, he was tempted to have a drink of the stronger stuff Connor kept under lock and key for special occasions—or so he claimed. But even in Blake's current state of mind he could acknowledge that drinking was not the way to approach this.

With his coffee in his hand, he walked to the window and looked out at the bustle of Cape Town on a Monday morning. The hotel overlooked parts of the business district, and he could feel the busyness of people trying to get somewhere rife in the air as he watched the relays of public transport. But he could also glimpse Table Mountain in the background, and he appreciated the simplicity of its magnitude. It somehow made him feel steadier as he thought about the state the hotel was in.

How had he let this happen?

The thought wouldn't leave his head. He had picked up that the hotel had been struggling years ago—which was why he had fired Landon and promoted Connor—but still this shouldn't have got past him. But he knew why it had. And he needed to be honest with himself before he blamed his employees when *he* was probably just as responsible for this mess.

He had been too focused on dealing with Julia to notice that the business was suffering.

His legs were restless now, as he got to the core of the problem, and he began to pace, coffee in hand, contemplating the situation. About five years ago the Elegance Hotel in Port Elizabeth had started losing staff at a high rate. When he'd noticed how low their retention numbers were, he'd arranged a meeting with HR to discuss it.

It had been at that meeting that he'd first met Julia.

She hadn't seemed to care that he was her boss, and had pushed the boundaries of what he had considered appropriate professional behaviour. But the reasons she had given him for losing staff had been right, and he'd had to acknowledge that she was an asset to their team. And as soon as he had she'd given him the smile that had drawn him in. Bright, bold, beautiful.

To this day, whenever he thought about that smile he felt a knock to his heart. Especially since those thoughts were so closely intertwined with the way it had softened when she'd looked at her son. The boy who had reminded him eerily of himself, and made him think about how Julia was giving him something Blake never had—a mother.

Until one day it had all shattered into the pieces that still haunted him.

He knew that Julia had taken his attention away from the hotels. And now this hotel was paying the price of a mistake he'd made before he'd known better. The thought conjured up Callie's face in his mind, but he forced it away, hoping to forget the way her eyes lit up her face when she smiled. He had just remembered the reason he didn't want to be attracted to her. He didn't want to be distracted either, and she had the word *distraction* written all over her beautiful face. *And*, he reminded himself again, he knew better now.

He grunted at the thought, walked back to the desk, and began to make some calls.

And ignored the face of the woman he had only met a few days ago as it drifted around in his head.

'Yes, darling, include that in my trip. I would *love* to see the mountain everyone keeps harping on about. And please include some cultural museums on my tour.' The woman sniffed, and placed a dignified hand on the very expensive pearls she wore around her neck. 'I can't only be doing *touristy* things, you know.'

'Of course, Mrs Applecombe.' Callie resisted the urge to tell the woman that visiting museums was very much a 'touristy' thing. 'I'll draw up a package for you and have it sent to your room by the end of the day. If you agree, we can arrange for the tour to be done the day after tomorrow.'

'Delightful.' Mrs Applecombe clasped her hands together. 'I just *know* Henry will love what we've discussed. Just remember, dear, that it's—'

'Supposed to be a surprise. I know.' Callie smiled, and stood. 'I'll make sure that it's everything you could hope for and more.'

After a few more lengthy reminders about the surprise anniversary gift for her husband Mrs Applecombe finally left, and Callie sighed in relief. She loved the woman's spirit, but after forty minutes of going back and forth about a tour Callie knew she could have designed in her sleep, she needed a break.

Luckily it was one o'clock, which meant she

could take lunch. But instead of sneaking into the kitchen, as she did most days, she locked the door to her office and flopped down on the two-seater couch she'd crammed into the small space so that if her guests wanted to they could be slightly more comfortable.

It had been a long morning. She'd done a quick tour first thing when she'd got in, followed by meetings with three guests wanting to plan trips. Usually she would be ecstatic about it. She loved her job. And she had Connor to thank for that.

She sighed, and sank even lower on the couch. Officially she was the 'Specialised Concierge'— a title she had initially thought pretentious, but one that seemed to thrill many of the more elite guests she worked with at the hotel. Unofficially she was a glorified tour guide, whose brother had persuaded her to work at the hotel to drag her from the very dark place she had been in after their parents' deaths.

She didn't have to think back that far to acknowledge that the job had saved her from that dark place. Once she had seen her parents' coffins descend into the ground—once she had watched people say their farewells and return to their lives as usual—she had found herself slipping. And even though her brother had been close to broken himself, he had stepped up and had helped her turn her life into something she knew had been out of her grasp after the car crash that had destroyed the life she had known and the people she loved.

The thought made her miss him terribly, and she grabbed her handbag and headed to Connor's office. Maybe he felt like having lunch together, and he could calm the ache that had suddenly started in her heart.

As she walked the short distance to his office she greeted some of the guests she recognised and nodded politely at those she didn't. She smiled in sympathy when she saw her friend Kate, dealing with a clearly testy guest at the front desk, and laughed when Kate mimicked placing a gun to her head as the guest leaned down to sign something.

Connor's door was slightly ajar when she got there, and she paused before knocking when she heard voices.

'If we keep doing what we're doing, in a couple of years—three, max—the hotel will be turning a profit again, Blake.' Connor's voice sounded panicked. 'I'm just not sure *this* plan is the best option. Surely there's something else we can do? Especially after we've stepped up in the last few years.'

'Connor, no one is denying the work you've done at the hotel. You've increased turnover by fifty per cent since you took over—which is saying something when you consider the state Landon left it in. But three years is too long to have a business running in the red.' There was a pause, and then Blake continued. 'Would you rather we move on to the other option? I've told you that it would come with a lot more complications...'

'Of course I would prefer *any* other option. But you know what's best for the hotel.'

Callie felt a trickle of unease run through her when she heard her brother's voice. It wasn't panicked this time, but resigned, as though he had given up hope on something.

'All right, then.' There was a beat of silence. 'I suppose we should start preparing to lay off staff.'

The words were fatalistic, and yet it took Callie a while to process what she had heard. Once she did, her legs moved without her consent and she burst through the office door.

'No!' she said, and her voice sounded as though it came from faraway. 'I can't let you do that.'

CHAPTER THREE

'EXCUSE ME?' BLAKE LIFTED his eyebrows, and suddenly Callie wished her tongue had given her the chance to think before she spoke.

'I'm so sorry, Mr Owen... Connor...' She saw the look in her brother's eyes and hoped her own apologised for interrupting. 'I just heard—'

'A *private* business conversation between members of management. Do you make a habit of eavesdropping?'

His eyes were steel, and she could hear the implication that he thought she had more poor habits than just eavesdropping.

'No, of course not. I was on my way to ask Connor if he'd like to do lunch, and then I heard you because the door was open.' She gestured behind her, although the action was useless now, since it stood wide open after her desperate entrance. 'I didn't mean to listen, but I did, and I'm telling you that you *can't* lay off staff. Please.'

Blake's handsome face softened slightly, and she cursed herself for noticing how his dark blue suit made him look like a model from the pages of a fashion magazine. It was probably the worst time to think of that, she thought, and instead focused on making some kind of case to make him reconsider.

'There are people here who need their jobs. Who *love* their jobs.' She could hear the plea in her voice. 'Employees here who have families who depend on them.'

'I'm aware of that, Miss McKenzie.' Blake frowned. 'I've thought every option through. This one is the best for the hotel. If we downsize now we can focus on operations and then expand again once we turn enough profit. It would actually be fairly simple.'

'For you, maybe. And for the hotel, sure. But I can assure you it would be anything but simple for the people you lay off—' She broke off, her heart pounding at the prospect. 'This is a business decision without any consideration for your employees.'

His eyes narrowed. 'I *have* considered my employees, and I resent your implication otherwise.

You have no idea what any other option would require from us. This is the most efficient way to help Elegance, Cape Town, get back on its feet.'

'Are you listening to yourself?' she asked desperately. 'You've been tossing around words like "downsizing" and "efficiency" as though those are *good* things. They aren't!'

'Callie—'

Connor stepped forward and she immediately felt ashamed of her behaviour when she saw the warning in his eyes. She knew she was embarrassing him in front of their boss. She even knew that she was embarrassing *herself* in front of her boss. So, even though more words tumbled through her mind, and even though the shame she felt was more for Connor than for herself, she stopped talking.

'It's okay, Connor.' Blake eased his way into one of the chairs in front of Connor's desk. 'I understand your sister's anger. However unprofessional.'

Callie's heart hammered in her chest and she wished that she hadn't said anything. But then she thought of Kate, and Connor, and of the fact that her job meant the world to her, and she straightened her shoulders. She wouldn't feel bad for standing up for their jobs. Not when it meant that she'd at least tried to save them.

'There is another option, Callie.'

Blake spoke quietly, and she wondered if he knew the power his voice held even so.

'I've looked into other investors.'

'Why did you dismiss the idea?'

Something shifted in his eyes, as though he hadn't expected her to ask him about his reasons.

'The Elegance hotels are the product of my father's hard work, and mine, and I don't want an outside investor to undermine that. Not at this stage of the game.'

He looked at her, and what she saw in his eyes gave her hope.

'Of course I *have* considered it. Especially an international investor, since that might give Elegance the boost it needs to go international. But it would be a very complicated process, and it would require a lot of negotiation.' He turned now, and looked at Connor. 'Like I told you before, I would have to think through the terms of this thoroughly before I make any decision.'

'But you'll reconsider it?' There was no disguising the hope Callie felt.

Blake looked at her, and those blue-green eyes were stormier than she had thought possible.

'I don't want another investor. This hotel group has been in my family for decades, Miss McKenzie. It's a legacy I want to pass on to my children.' He paused. 'But if we can secure an international investor, that legacy might be even more than I thought possible. We'll talk about it.'

He gestured to Connor, and then moved to sit behind the desk Connor had had put in his office for Blake.

Callie waited, but the look on her brother's face told her she had been dismissed. She nearly skipped out of the room, because despite his noncommittal response Blake Owen *was* considering an option other than laying off staff. If Blake chose an investor it would mean that everything her brother had worked so hard for wouldn't have been for nothing.

He had toiled night and day to try and get the hotel running smoothly again, and the news of Blake's arrival had been a difficult pill to swallow—it had been a clear sign that everything

Connor had done hadn't been enough. Callie knew he loved the hotel, and the last thing that he wanted was for his employees to lose their jobs. And, she thought, the last thing *she* wanted was for him to lose his job—and for her to lose hers.

So before she left she wanted to say one more thing to Blake.

'Mr Owen… Blake?'

He looked up, and she smiled.

'Thank you for reconsidering.'

Blake couldn't sleep. He had been working with Connor until just past midnight, trying to draft an investment contract that he was happy with. A contract that would require all his negotiation skills to convince an investor to accept—although he knew it was possible. He had put out feelers even before he had spoken to Connor, when he had initially thought of finding an investor, and the response had been positive. But he still wasn't convinced that this was something he wanted or if it was something he was being persuaded into by a pretty face.

He threw off his bedcovers and walked downstairs to the kitchen of his Cape Town house. He had bought the place without much thought other than that he would need somewhere to stay when he visited his father, who had retired here. Now he was incredibly grateful he had, since he didn't know how long he would be in town.

The house was a few kilometres from the hotel, and had an amazing view. He could even see the lights of the city illuminating Table Mountain at night through the glass doors that led out onto a deck on the second floor. But he wasn't thinking about that as he poured himself a glass of water and drank as though he had come out of a desert.

Since the house was temperature-controlled, he knew he wasn't feeling the heat of the January weather. No, he thought. It was because he was considering something that would complicate his life when all he'd wanted was a simple solution.

Blake had been raised in the family business. His father had opened the first Elegance Hotel four decades ago, and had invested heavily in guest relations. He had made sure that every employee knew that the Elegance Hotel's guests came first, and seen that vision manifested into action. Eventually, after two decades, his investment had paid off and he had been able to expand into other hotels.

Blake had been groomed to take over since he was old enough to understand that his father was not only building a business, but a legacy. And he hadn't been given control of the hotel until his father had been sure that he could do it.

That was why he wanted to lay off staff instead of considering an outside investor. He would be able to solve the problem that had arisen while he'd been trying to fix his relationship with Julia easily, and make the reminder of his failure disappear. It would mean that his feelings of losing control and being helpless would be gone.

A memory of himself standing at the front door, watching his mother leave, flashed through his mind, but he shook it away, not knowing where it had come from, and forced his thoughts back to the matter at hand. Laying off staff might have been the simple option, but it was also a selfish one. Especially when he thought of the hope he had seen written on Callie and Connor's faces.

He sighed as he made his decision. He would do this—but not for Callie. The slight heat that flushed through him every time he thought about her, the intensity of it every time he saw her, was a sure sign that he should stay away from her. He *wouldn't* make this big a decision based on his attraction to her or her need for him to do so. He wouldn't make that mistake again.

'Mr Owen, do you have a moment?'

Callie stood awkwardly at the door, wishing with all her might that she didn't feel quite so small in his presence. But she straightened when he looked up and gestured for her to come in.

She knew Connor had to attend one of the conferences at the hotel today, and she was using the opportunity to speak to her boss without her brother's disapproving look. And without the disapproving lecture she would no doubt receive—like the one she'd received just after midnight—which, she had been told, was when Connor and Blake had finally finished their meeting.

She knew she'd been out of line when she had spoken up, and she hadn't needed Connor to tell her that. So once again she was preparing to apologise to Blake.

She walked in and swallowed when he looked

up, the striking features of his face knitted into a stern expression.

'What can I do for you, Miss McKenzie?'

'It's Callie, please.'

He nodded. 'Okay, then. What can I do for you, Callie?'

Her stomach jilted just a little at the way he said her name. She cleared her throat. 'I wanted to say sorry.'

He almost smiled. 'It's becoming a habit, then.'

She let out a laugh. 'Seems like it. I've made quite the mess since meeting you.' She stepped forward, resisted pulling at her clothes. 'But I *am* sorry. The first time I apologised it was because I'd made a mistake. This time it's because I shouldn't have barged in here and spoken out of turn.'

'I'm not upset with you because you spoke out of turn.'

Blake stood, walked around the desk and leaned against it. He was wearing a blue shirt, and the top button was loosened. She swallowed, and wondered if the temperature in the room had increased.

'I'm not your school principal.'

'Aren't you, though? In some ways?'

This time he did smile, and it did something strange to her heart.

'I won't take the bait on that one.'

He paused, and then crossed his arms. She could see the muscle ripple under his shirt, and the heat went up another notch.

'You say you're sorry for barging in here. But not that you eavesdropped?'

'No, I'm not sorry about that. If I hadn't you wouldn't have considered investors. Which you *have* been doing, right?' she asked, and knew that subtlety was not her forte.

'I have. I made a few calls this morning, and I have a few people interested.'

He walked towards her, and though the distance between them wasn't small her heart thudded.

'So the answer to your real question is yes, I am going to do this.'

'You *are*?' Relief washed over her. 'Oh, wow!' She pressed a hand to her stomach. 'That's amazing.'

'But I need your help.'

Relief turned into confusion. 'What do you mean?'

'Like I said yesterday, we need a very specific kind of investor. An international one who will be willing to invest in the hotel, but also in this city. Especially if I want him to agree to my strict terms regarding the expansion of Elegance Hotels.'

His hands were in his pockets now, and he moved until he was just close enough that she could smell his cologne. It reminded her of when they were in the elevator together—a time when she hadn't had to think of him as her boss.

She shook off the feelings the memory evoked, but when she spoke, her voice was a little husky. 'And how can I help with that?'

'You can help me sell the city. You are the "Specialised Concierge", right?'

He smiled slyly, and she realised he knew about her made-up title.

'Or, in more common terms, a tour guide,' she said.

'Exactly. So I'll need you to help me sell Cape Town to potential investors. Your knowledge of the city will be an asset to any proposal I make. I'll take care of the business side of it, of course, and once that's done we can take them on the tour you will custom-design to fit my proposal.'

'How do you know I can do it?' She felt her heart beat in a rhythm that couldn't possibly be healthy.

'Because your job depends on it.'

He smiled now, and she couldn't read the emotion that lined it.

'Callie, are you prepared to work with the boss?'

She stared helplessly at him, and despite everything inside her that nudged her to say otherwise she answered, 'Yes, I am.'

CHAPTER FOUR

'YOU'RE HERE BECAUSE you want to keep your job. You're here because you want to save Connor's job. You're here because you're saving your colleagues' jobs.'

Callie repeated the words to herself as she walked into what had previously been known as Conference Room A. Blake had turned it into an office. Not one he would share with Connor. No, that had ended the minute she had agreed to work with him. This conference-room-turned-office was hers and Blake's to share. It was one of their medium-sized conference rooms, and Callie had only been in it a few times when she'd had tours with groups of more than six. But, despite its reasonable size, Callie felt closed in. And this time she wasn't fooling herself by attributing the feeling to claustrophobia.

Her heart hammered as she saw him sitting at one end of the rectangular table, a large whiteboard behind him already half filled with illegible writing.

'Are you sure you weren't meant to be a doctor?' she asked, hoping to break the tension she felt within herself.

Blake looked up at her, his eyes sharp despite how hard she knew he had been working. The hotel had been rife with the news that Blake had been holed up in the conference room for the entire week it had taken for Callie to sort out her schedule. She'd done her tours for that week, but had cancelled everything beyond that. Blake had made it very clear that Callie's full attention would be needed for the investors, and that was what she was doing.

She tilted her head when he grabbed a cup of what Callie assumed had once been coffee from in front of him. By the look on his face, it was something significantly less desirable now.

'I'll get you some more,' she said, and placed her files and handbag a few seats away from his.

This was their first official day of working together, and Callie wasn't sure what it would be like to work with the boss. She was already distracted by being alone with him in the same room, she thought as she poured coffee into two cups that sat on the counter along one side of the conference room. The hotel staff had made sure that everything their boss could possibly need was in that room.

She'd heard them whispering amongst themselves, and had taken it upon herself to defuse their curiosity.

'We're going to try and save the hotel,' she'd told Kate, knowing her friend couldn't keep a secret for the life of her, 'and if we do things will stay the same for the foreseeable future.'

Since she'd let that little titbit go, her colleagues had done everything in their power to make sure they had the fuel to save the hotel. And maybe the world, she thought, and wrinkled her nose at the extensive display of pastries that lined the rest of the counter.

'How many people are eating this?' she wondered out loud, and set the coffee in front of Blake.

'Two today.' He sighed as he sipped from the coffee. 'It's been like that ever since I started working in here. I think they think I'm a competitive eater in my spare time.'

She laughed. 'Or a man who needs as much energy as possible so that he can work to save their jobs.' He frowned, and she elaborated. 'People were getting restless about what you being here means. I told a friend, and she told everyone else. Trust me—it's better this way. Otherwise they might have been planning to starve you instead of feed you.'

She grinned, and felt herself relax. This wasn't so bad. They were having a normal conversation. Just as she would with any of her colleagues. But then Blake smiled in return, and her heart thumped with that incredibly fast rhythm she was beginning to think was personalised for him. Like a ringtone.

She cleared her throat. 'How's everything going here?'

'Good.' He took another sip of the coffee, and settled back in his chair. 'I've created interest amongst my contacts by highlighting how beneficial it would be for them to be a part of my business, so we're looking at a few potential prospects.'

She stared at him. 'You're good.'

He grinned at her. 'Thanks. It's going to be

a lot easier for both of us now that you've re-alised that.'

She felt her lips twitch. 'It's a good thing I have, then. Now, what do you need from *me*, Mr Owen?'

'Blake,' he said, and shrugged when she frowned. 'I feel like my father every time you call me that.'

'Fine,' she said, and forced herself to say his name without feeling anything. 'Blake, what do you need from me?'

There was a pause as the question settled between them, and it made her feel as though she'd said something inappropriate. And the way he looked at her made her feel like she wanted to give him whatever he thought he needed from her—even if it wasn't something that was strictly professional. She exhaled slowly, and hoped that the tension inside her would seep out with her breath. It did—but only because he finally responded.

'Well, we need to start working on a proposal. But, since I'm still at the stage of securing possible investors, please start drawing up a list of places you think we can include in the tour portion of the proposal. Include your motivations for why you think we should visit them. We can take it from there.'

'Okay,' she said, and then frowned when he grabbed his coffee and hung the tie that had been carelessly thrown across his chair over his shoulder. 'Where are you going?'

'To work in Connor's office for a while. Just so we don't disturb each other while I'm busy with my calls.'

He nodded at her, and then left her wondering why he had asked her to work with him in the conference room when he wouldn't even be there.

'Welcome back,' Callie said later, as Blake entered the room.

'Thanks.' He nodded, and opted for a glass of water instead of the coffee he knew he should take a break from. Especially since his throat was nearly raw from all the talking he had been doing for the last few hours.

He had been successful—had spoken to many of the parties who had contacted him—and he could no longer justify staying away from the conference room. Not when he had insisted Callie work with him and that they should do things together.

'What do you have so far?'

Callie gave him a measured look, and immediately he felt chastised that he hadn't made small talk first. But he didn't trust himself to do that just yet. Not while he was still trying to convince himself that working with her had been a *business* decision, and had nothing to do with the way she made him feel. Especially after he had told himself that he would stay away from her.

Even now, as she sat poised behind the table, her white shirt snug enough for him to see curves he didn't want to notice, he could feel a pull between them that had nothing to do with business.

And it scared him.

'Well, I've done exactly as you asked. I've drawn up a list of must-see locations that I think we should consider for your proposal.'

She stood and handed him the list, and he saw that her black trousers were still as neat as they had been that morning, when she'd first walked in. She looked pristine—even though, based on the papers in his hands, she had been working extensively on her planning.

'You can have a look at them and let me know what you think, but I don't think there will be a problem with any of them. I've also tentatively set up some tour ideas.'

Blake struggled to get over the way her proximity threatened to take over his senses, but he forced it to the back of his mind and listened to her explain some of the ideas she'd had. As she did, his own began to form. A business proposal that would complement what she had in mind. But he didn't know if it would work without seeing it first.

'Okay—great.' He put down his glass of water and gestured towards the chair where her jacket lay. 'Grab your things and we can go immediately.'

'What?' Her eyes widened.

'I want you to show me these must-see locations. I mean, what you have is great—theoretically—but I need you to show them to me so that I know they work in practice.'

'And you want to go right now?'

'Yes.' He walked to the door and opened it for her. 'The longer we wait, the longer we delay finalising plans. And that's not the way I work.'

Callie stood staring at him, as though at any minute he was going to say, *Just joking!* When she realised that it wasn't going to happen, she grabbed her jacket and handbag and walked past him through the open door.

Her scent was still as enticing as it had been that first night, and for a brief moment—not for the first time—Blake wondered if he was making a mistake. He had asked her to work with him on impulse, although he had known it was a logical, even smart way of approaching the international investor angle once he'd had a chance to think about it. So why was it that he'd avoided working with her for the entire morning if he was so convinced that it was all business between them?

It didn't matter, he thought, and shook away any lingering doubts. He had a job to do. And that job would come first.

Callie waited as John, the parking valet, pulled up in Blake's silver sedan. This evidence of his wealth jostled her, though she knew she shouldn't be surprised. Of *course* her boss had money, she thought, and watched Blake thank John and wave him away when the valet moved to open the door for her. Instead, Blake did it himself, and she got in, her skin prickling when she brushed against him by accident.

She ignored it, instead focusing on the car. It was just as luxurious on the inside as it was on the outside—as she'd expected—with gadgets that she didn't quite think were necessary. But, then again, she drove an old second-hand car that made her arms ache every time she had to turn the wheel. Perhaps if she had thought about gadgets, she wouldn't have to worry that her car might stall every time she drove it.

Nevertheless, she was proud of the little thing. It was the first car she'd ever bought, and she'd worked incredibly hard since leaving high school and saved every last rand to buy it. Granted, she'd worked for her parents, and she knew they had been liberal in their payment.

She smiled at the memory, and caught her breath when he asked, 'What's that for?'

She hadn't realised he was paying attention to her. She should have known better. *Always be on guard*, she reminded herself.

'I was just admiring your car. And comparing

it with mine. It doesn't,' she said with a smile when he gave her a questioning look.

'I bought it when I knew I was coming to Cape Town. I had no idea how long I was going to be here, and I didn't want to impose on my father and use one of his indefinitely. I'll probably sell it as soon as I know where I'm going next.'

Though her heart stuck on the information that he would be leaving, she asked, 'You didn't own a car before?'

'I did. But I sold it a while ago—when I realised I would be travelling a lot more.'

'But don't you need one for when you're at home?'

He took a right turn and glanced over to her. 'I don't have a home.'

For some reason Callie found that incredibly sad. 'I'm sorry.'

'Don't be. It's a choice.'

She wanted to ask him why, but the silence that stretched between them made it clear that he didn't want to reveal the reasons for that choice. She respected that. There were things she wouldn't want to reveal to him either.

'Blake, shouldn't *I* be driving?'

He frowned. 'Why? Can't you direct me to where we're going?'

'I can, but that won't give you the experience we'd be giving potential investors. And that's what you want, isn't it? That's why we're here?'

'I suppose so.' He signalled and pulled off to the side of the road.

They switched seats, and for a moment Callie just enjoyed the sleekness of the car. A car *she* would be driving for the day. She resisted the urge to giggle—and then the urge disappeared when she became aware of the other things sitting on the driver's side meant. The heat of his body was almost embedded into the seat. She could smell him. She traced her hands over the steering wheel, thinking how his had been there only a few moments ago.

She cleared her throat, willing the heat she felt through her body to go away. After putting on her safety belt, she pulled back into the road and aligned her thoughts. But they stuck when she realised he was looking at her.

'What?' she asked nervously. 'Am I doing something wrong?'

'No.' He smiled, and it somewhat eased the

tension between them. 'I just didn't think this was how the day would turn out. You driving me around in my car.'

'Are you disappointed?' Callie turned left, a plan forming in her mind for their day. It was more of an outline, but she was sure it would suffice for something so last-minute.

'No. You're doing quite a remarkable job—especially considering I'm not a fan of being a passenger.'

'Really?' She glanced over in surprise. 'I thought you would be used to being chauffeured.'

'When the need arises, yes. But I try to keep those occasions to the minimum.'

'Because you like to be the one in control?'

He frowned, and for a minute Callie thought she had gone too far.

'Maybe, though I think it has more to do with my father. He loves his cars, and couldn't wait to share that love with me. So I like to drive him when I can so we can talk about something other than the hotel.'

Callie felt her heart ache at the revelation she didn't think Blake knew he had let slip. And, though a part of her urged her to accept the information about his relationship with his father without comment, she couldn't help but say, 'It must have made him proud that you took over his legacy. The hotels,' she elaborated when she felt his questioning glance. 'I read the article *Corporate Times* did on the two of you when he retired.'

She didn't mention that she'd read it—and many others—just a few weeks ago, when she'd heard Blake would be coming to Cape Town. When he didn't respond, she looked over and saw a puzzled expression on his face. Nerves kicked in and she felt the babbling that would come from her mouth before it even started.

'I just meant that he must be proud of you since he loved the hotel business so much. And since you're also, in some ways, his legacy, it's like his legacy running his legacy...' She shook her head at how silly that sounded. 'Anyway, that's why I said he must be proud.'

Blake didn't respond, and she wondered if she'd upset him. She should probably just have left it alone, she thought as she drove up the inclined road that led to Table Mountain. But it wasn't as if she was prying. Okay, maybe it was. But she'd only said something she thought was true. Surely he couldn't fault her for that?

'I think you might be right.'

He spoke so softly that she was grateful the radio was off or she might have missed it.

'He doesn't talk about it much, but I think maybe he is.'

Callie nodded, and was amazed at how those few words confirmed what she'd suspected earlier about his relationship with his father. She considered pressing for more information, but he asked her a question before she could.

'Where are you taking me first?'

She bit her lip to prevent her questions about his family from tumbling out. 'Table Mountain. Our number one tourist attraction, and also an incredible experience if you live here. This would be the first place I'd want to see if I hadn't been to Cape Town before.' She frowned. 'But, since you *have* been to Cape Town before, I'm sure this trip is redundant for you.'

'No. I haven't been up the mountain.'

He shrugged when she shot him an incredulous look.

'I've only been here for business or to visit my family. I don't do touristy things.'

'But…' She found herself at a loss for words. 'Don't you and your family go out together? I mean, this is the best outing for a family.'

'For certain kinds of families, yes, I suppose it is. But our family isn't one of those.'

Again, Callie felt an incredible grief at his words. They'd been driving for less than twenty minutes and already she knew that Blake didn't know if his father was proud of him or not, that their conversations mostly revolved around business, and that his family didn't do outings together.

She didn't know what was worse, she realised as she parked. Having a family—parents—and not having a great relationship with them, or having no parents but wonderful memories of them. She had always known that her parents were proud of her. And suddenly, for the first time since they'd died, she was grateful for those memories she had of her parents, no longer pushing them away.

CHAPTER FIVE

'IT'S BEAUTIFUL, ISN'T IT?'

Callie's voice was soft next to him, and he turned slightly to her, not wanting to move his eyes from the view.

'I don't think I've ever seen anything like it,' he said, knowing that the words couldn't be more true.

They stood at the top of Table Mountain, looking over the city and the harbour. If he walked to the other side, he knew he'd see the beaches and the ocean in a way he'd never experienced before. They weren't the only ones up there, but for the peace Blake felt he thought that they might as well be. He didn't think about failure or disappointment here. He felt so small, so insignificant, that thinking about his own problems seemed selfish.

Though he'd just done it, he walked back to the other side of the mountain and looked down at the ocean. There were houses scattered across the peaks of the hills above it, and he felt a tug of jealousy that the residents there were privy to such a spectacular view every day of their lives.

'I wonder if those people know how lucky they are to live there,' he said, aware that Callie was standing right next to him.

From the moment they'd stepped into the cable car to get up the mountain she'd left him to his thoughts. Thoughts that were tangled around her and her questions about his family. He hadn't wanted to talk about it, and he thought she'd realised as much when she'd remained quiet after her last question about going out as a family. But even though she was silent he had never been more aware of her presence. That peaceful, steady presence that he hadn't expected.

'Well, most of them are rich tycoons who purchase those houses and rent them out. Some are wealthy Cape Townians who invest or buy just because they can.' She paused, seemed almost hesitant to continue. 'And others are very aware of how lucky they are.'

'You know some of the others?'

'You could say so.' A ghost of a smile shadowed her lips. 'I live there.'

He struggled not to gape at her, but he couldn't resist the words. 'You *live* there?'

'Yes.'

The smile was full-blown now, and it warmed something inside him that he had thought was frozen.

'Right over there.'

She pointed, and he wondered which of the spectacular houses was hers.

'Connor said he lives in one of the main parts of town.'

'*He* does, yes. But we don't live together. He moved out of the house when he went to university. My parents were devastated, but they had me, and I had no plans for moving out. I commuted to university for my first year and then...' She trailed off and cleared her throat. 'And now I still live there.'

Her words made him want to ask so many questions. He wanted to break through whatever barrier she'd put up and find out why she hadn't continued with her story. Instead he settled for one of his many questions.

'Alone?'

She looked at him, and the pain in her eyes nearly stole his breath.

'Alone.'

Silence stretched between them while Blake tried to find words to comfort a hurt he didn't know anything about. But words failed him, and all he could do was wait helplessly.

'Come on—there's a lot more to show you,' she said, after what felt like for ever, and he followed her back to the cable car.

Somewhere in the back of his mind he was reminded that they were there for business, and as soon as the thought registered he took his phone from his pocket. He opened a memo and recorded Table Mountain as an approved place for the investors to see.

'This must be a really popular place for your tours,' he said as the cable car began its descent.

'It is.'

Was that relief he heard in her voice?

'I usually begin here or end here. Ending here usually works when the tour starts in the afternoon and we can make it up the mountain for sunset.'

'I'd love to see that.'

She smiled. 'It's definitely something to see. Maybe some day I'll take you.'

They were simple words, but Blake felt them shift something inside him. An emotion he hadn't experienced until he'd met her jolted him. *Hope.* He hadn't hoped for anything in a long time. Nor had he thought he would want to watch the sunset on top of a mountain with a woman who made him feel things he didn't want to feel.

'Where to next?' he asked when they reached the car.

'That, Mr Owen, would take all the fun out of today.'

She grinned, and he felt himself smiling back, despite what he was fighting inside.

'If Table Mountain is included in a morning tour I usually schedule it for about ten. We'd usually end there at about twelve, and then either have lunch at the top of the mountain or take a drive down to Camps Bay to have lunch.'

She nearly purred at the way the car was handling the curves of the road.

'I usually prefer driving down, because then

our guests get to experience this amazing drive. And once there they can have lunch at one of the many upper-class but affordable restaurants.'

'I can't fault you on that,' Blake said, and she glanced over to see he was looking out of the window. 'This view is amazing.'

'I know.'

She smiled, and thought that her tour wasn't going badly. She hadn't shown him much yet, but she wanted to take him to the places she knew would provide opportunities to market the hotel to his investors. And she hadn't been able to resist showing him the best attraction—Table Mountain—first.

'If they like it, I tell them they can stay at the beach for the afternoon and we'll send a shuttle to fetch them when they're ready.'

'Sounds like a tourist's dream.'

'It is,' she agreed. 'Although, to be fair, it's a resident's dream as well.'

'The grateful ones.'

He looked at her and smiled, and she had to force her eyes back to the road.

'If you live here, you must drive this road every day?'

'Mostly, yes,' she said, and thanked her heart for returning to its usual pace. 'But I live further up, so I wouldn't take this part of the road. It leads to the beach,' she continued, when she realised he was probably just as much of a tourist in Cape Town as her guests were.

'Do you often go to the beach?'

She slowed down as they turned onto the road along the beachfront. 'Probably once a week. Never to swim or tan.' She smiled and drove into an underground car park. 'I usually go in the evenings for a run or a walk. It helps clear my head.'

They got out, and she suddenly realised that she hadn't told him she thought they should have lunch. Self-doubt kicked in, and she said nervously, 'Um…there isn't really much to do here unless you have your swimming trunks hidden under your suit.'

She flushed when she realised what she had said. Even more so when she thought about him in swimming gear.

'But I *can* introduce you to the management at some of the restaurants the hotel guests usually frequent during the tours. And we can grab lunch on our way to the next stop.'

She didn't wait for his response but instead led the way to the beachfront, where the line of restaurants was. The idea of sitting down and having lunch with him was still slightly terrifying to her, so she was taking the easy way out.

As she introduced Blake to the different restaurateurs she watched him slip into a professional mode that oozed charm and sophistication. He asked the right questions, said the right things, and ensured that everyone respected him. Which meant that many of them—whom Callie knew quite well—were now even more interested in the Elegance Hotel, having met its CEO. And they genuinely seemed to like him.

She grudgingly admitted that it made *her* like him a little more, too, but told herself that she was talking about her boss—not the man she'd met in the elevator.

Desperately trying to distract herself, she asked if he'd like to eat and then took him to one of stores that did takeaway wraps and salads. They ordered, and stood in silence. Callie waited for him to say something—anything—about all the people they'd spoken to, but instead he sat down at one of the tables and stared out at the ocean.

She joined him, and yet the silence continued. When she couldn't take it any more she asked, 'So, do you like the beach?'

Callie knew it wasn't her best shot, but the silence had made her observant, and the more she observed, the more she responded to Blake. She felt the movement of her heart, the heat in her body, but she refused to succumb to them. She just wanted to talk, to take her mind off what being in his presence did to her.

'Who doesn't?'

His eyes didn't move from the ocean, but she could see a slight smile on his lips.

'I didn't go nearly as much as I would have liked to when I was younger. And when I took over the hotels there just wasn't time. I don't know when I was last at a beach like this.'

'You should make the time.' She offered a tentative smile when he glanced back at her. 'At both our stops so far you've seemed...I don't know...at peace with the world.' She blushed when he turned his body so that he was facing her. 'I just think that if something makes you feel at peace, makes you happy, you should make the time for it.'

He didn't respond for a while, and Callie bit her lip in fear that she might have said the wrong thing. His eyes lowered to her lips then, and the heat she'd felt earlier was nothing compared to what flowed through her body at his gaze. If he had been anyone else she would have leaned forward and kissed him. But he wasn't anyone else, and she couldn't look away when he looked back into her eyes.

'What do *you* make time for, Callie McKenzie? What makes you happy or makes you feel peaceful?'

The question would have been innocent if he hadn't still been looking at her as if she was the only woman on earth.

She cleared her throat. 'Gardening. I garden.'

Blake tilted his head with a frown, and then grinned. 'I would never have guessed that.'

She smiled back at him, grateful that the tension between them had abated. 'I don't blame you. I'm terrible at it. I buy things and plant them, but mostly I pay someone to look after them.'

He laughed, and Callie couldn't believe how attracted she was to him when he looked so carefree. 'So you plant things but don't look after them? And that makes you happy?'

She nodded, remembering the first time she had done it.

'Yes, it does. It reminds me of my mother. We used to do it together—though I was just as bad then as I am now.' She stared out to the ocean, memories making her forget where she was. Who she was with. 'But my mom would just let me plant, and then she'd fix what I did wrong. When I was old enough to realise, I asked her why she let me do it.' She looked down, barely noticing how her hands played with the end of her top. 'She told me that it was because it made me happy, and that if something makes you happy you should do it.'

She looked up at him and saw compassion in his eyes, before she realised that tears had filled her own. She lifted her head, embarrassed and raw from what she'd told him, the way she'd reacted, and only looked back at him when she was sure she had her emotions under control.

He took a hand from her lap and squeezed it,

but before he could say what he clearly wanted to their order number was called.

They grabbed their lunch and without saying anything ate as they walked back to the car.

She wasn't sure what had prompted her to tell him that. Maybe it had been the moment...the setting. But the more likely answer—the one she didn't want to consider—was that maybe it was *him*. He made her feel things—things she would fight as long as she could. Feeling safe enough, secure enough to open up to someone would take a lot more than just a few hours with him.

And it wouldn't be with her boss. No, she thought as she threw away her half-eaten wrap. She couldn't open up to her boss.

Blake had wanted to say something to her from the moment she had told him about her mother. He wanted to comfort her, tell her that it was okay that she'd told him, that the fear and surprise he'd seen in her eyes when she'd realised what she'd said wasn't necessary. But instead, like the coward he was, he stayed silent and went along with the rest of the tour as though she *hadn't* just let him see such an intimate part of herself.

On their way back from the beach she drove him up to the Bo-Kaap, where colourful houses lined the streets. She told him about the rich cultural heritage of the area—how it had come to be a place of refuge for the Islamic slaves who had been freed in 1834. She pointed out the museum that had been established over a century later, and had been designed according to the typical Muslim home in the nineteenth century.

'The design is in the process of changing at the moment, but the museum will tell you quite a lot about one of the most thriving cultural communities in Cape Town.' She turned the car around and drove back down the hill. 'You should make an effort to visit it some time.'

After that she took him to the V&A Waterfront—another cultural hub of the city. It was both a mall and a dock, he discovered as they walked past a mass of shoppers to get to the actual waterfront. The large boats there were either docked for repair or in to pick up cargo, and the smaller ones either belonged to private citizens or were available for hire.

They also transported people to Robben Island,

he discovered as he climbed into a boat and sat next to Callie.

Since it was the last trip of the day the boat was quite full, and he was forced to sit closer to her than he would have liked. Her perfume made him feel a need he had never felt before. Even mixed with the salty smell of the sea, its effect on him was potent. He wanted her to turn to him so that he could kiss her, just so that he could make his need for her subside.

He couldn't shake it off even when they arrived at the island where Nelson Mandela had famously spent twenty-seven years of his life. His thoughts were filled with her as the tour guide walked them through a typical day in the prison, as he told them about the ex-President of South Africa and showed them his cell.

By the time they had got back to the waterfront, it was late enough for their day to end. But he didn't want that. No, he didn't want the day to end. Because then he would have to go back to the hotel...back to being her boss.

'We should go for dinner,' he said, without fully realising it. 'It's been a long day and we've barely eaten. I think the least I can do for you after today is take you out.'

Her mouth opened and closed a few times, and his heart pounded at the prospect of her saying no. But then she answered him.

'Yeah…okay. Where do you want to go?'

'Somewhere you love.' He cleared his throat. 'I want to see more of Cape Town, but not just the side that your guests see.'

'Um…' She looked lost for a second, and then she nodded. 'Okay, I'll take you to one of my favourite places. But you can drive this time.'

He nodded and climbed into the driver's seat, following her directions until she'd finished typing the location into his GPS.

'You weren't lying when you said you haven't seen much of Cape Town, were you?'

The question was so random that he didn't take the time to think his answer through. 'No. My father and stepmother moved here when he retired, which was about eight years ago. I've probably been here twice a year since then to see them, and a few more times for the hotel. But that's the extent of my travels to Cape Town.'

'Where did you live before?'

'Port Elizabeth, for the most part. But, like I mentioned, I travelled a lot between hotels.'

'Do you miss it? Port Elizabeth?'

He thought about telling her the truth—that he didn't miss being there because it reminded him of his relationship with Julia, and how he had failed at that and let his business down. But that would only open himself up to more questions, and force him to face things he didn't want to remember.

Luckily the GPS declared that they had arrived, and he used the opportunity to deflect the question.

'What *is* this place?'

She tilted her head, as though she knew what he was doing, but answered him.

'It's called Sakari—which means "sweet" in Inuit. They specialise in dessert and have the most delicious milkshakes—though the food is pretty incredible, too.'

They walked inside, and Blake took a moment to process the look of the restaurant. It wasn't big, but it comfortably fitted its customers without seeming stuffy. There were even a few couches in front of a fireplace. Since it was still summer, the fire wasn't lit, but the couches were filled with people ranging through all ages. The doors were open and a slight breeze filled the room, causing the candles that had been lit for atmosphere to flutter every now and then.

It was a perfect summer's evening, he thought, in a perfect—and intimate—restaurant. He shrugged off what the thought conjured inside him and returned his attention to the hostess, who was greeting Callie with a warmth that he'd never witnessed before.

'Hi, Bianca, how are you?'

Callie spoke to the hostess as though she were her best friend.

The woman had a full head of black and blue curls that complemented her gorgeous olive skin.

'Great, thanks. Ben and I just found out we're having a girl!'

Blake only then realised the woman was pregnant as he looked at the slight bump under her apron. He figured she was probably around four months, and waited as Callie congratulated Bianca and asked if she could squeeze them in.

'Of course. Give me a second.'

Callie turned to him and her eyes were bright.

'Bianca is my father's business partner's daughter. She opened this little restaurant about eight years ago. My dad was so proud of her—almost like she was his own.'

'Was...?'

'Yes.'

Her eyes dimmed, and suddenly he put together all the bits and pieces that she'd told him throughout the day. Her house, the almost-tears when she'd spoken about her mother, and now the past tense with her father. And just as quickly he realised he'd pressed her when he shouldn't have.

'Callie, I'm so sorry.'

CHAPTER SIX

'DON'T WORRY ABOUT IT.'

Callie cleared her throat and smiled when Bianca led them to a table in the corner. She knew the woman had probably squeezed it in herself, and she thanked her and rolled her eyes at the wink Bianca sent her after looking at Blake.

Callie busied herself with looking at the menu, and though she could feel him staring at her eventually Blake did the same. She sighed in relief, knowing that she didn't want to talk about her parents' deaths with him. She just wanted to have dinner and go home, where she would be safe from the feelings that stirred through her when she was with him.

'Their burgers are really good. And of course you should have one with a milkshake.'

She spoke because she didn't want to revert to their previous topic of conversation.

'Sounds good,' he said, and placed his menu

down. And then he asked exactly what she'd tried to prevent. 'When did you lose your parents?'

She didn't want to talk about this, she thought, and shut her eyes. But when she opened them again his own were filled with compassion and sincerity. So she gave him a brief answer. 'Almost a decade ago now.'

He nodded, and was silent for a bit. 'My mom left when I was eleven. It's not the same thing, of course, but I think I may understand a little of what you feel.'

She stared at him—not because his mom had left, but because he'd shared the fact with her. It made her feel—*comforted.* That was terrible, she thought, but then he smiled at her, and she realised that comforting her had been his intention. She found herself smiling back before she averted her eyes.

How did he *do* that? And in this place that was so personal to her? She'd brought him here out of instinct, because she'd honestly had no idea what else to do. He'd put her on the spot and the only place she'd been able to think of was the one her friend owned—the one she had so often come to with her father in the year before his death.

She tried to pop in as often as possible, even just to grab one of the chocolate croissants that Sakari was known for. Maybe it was because she didn't want to lose the connection she'd had with her father. But it had taken a long time after his death for her to realise that.

'I know this isn't what you're used to.' She changed the subject to a safer topic. 'I mean, it isn't a five-star restaurant or anything, but it is highly rated.'

He laughed. 'It isn't what I'm used to—but not because I'm a snob, which you seem to be implying.'

She blushed, because maybe he was right.

'I just don't have time to find places like this. I usually eat at the hotel, or go out to dinner for business.'

'Do you enjoy it?'

'My job?'

She smiled, and wondered if he knew how cute he looked when he was confused. 'No—being so busy.'

He didn't respond immediately, and when the waiter came to take their order he still hadn't said anything. She didn't press, because somehow she knew he was formulating his answer.

'It works for me.' He shrugged. 'Keeping busy means I don't have to think about the problems in my personal life.'

She hadn't expected such a candid answer, but she took the opportunity to say, 'Your family?'

He nodded, though he didn't look at her. 'Partly, yes. And some other things.'

Callie suddenly remembered what he'd said about dating, and how he had told her without words that a woman had made him cynical about it. As much as she wanted to know, she didn't ask. She didn't want to tell him about how her parents had died, or how she'd fallen apart when they had. And clearly there were things that *he* didn't want to speak to her about either. And that was fair. Though a part of her hoped that it would change.

'Well, I hope that one day, when this mess is all over, you'll take a day to relax.'

'Relax?'

'Yes, it's this thing us normal people do—usually in the evenings or over weekends—when we try to put aside thoughts of business and enjoy the moment.'

He leaned back in his seat and grinned. 'Never heard of it.'

She laughed. 'I could show you some time. It's pretty easy.'

'I'd like that.'

He spoke softly, and suddenly the noise in the restaurant faded to the background as she held his gaze. Thoughts of the two of them spending evenings together, weekends, made her heart pound. And yearn.

He lifted a hand and laid it over hers, and suddenly the sweetness of her thoughts turned to fire. She wanted to lean over, kiss him. She wanted to know what it would be like to feel his lips on hers, his hands on her body. His hand tightened on hers and she wondered if he knew her thoughts. The way his eyes heated as he looked at her made her think he did, and she leaned forward—just a bit. If this was going to happen, then she didn't want him only to be a spectator.

And then the waiter brought their milkshakes, told them their burgers were about ten minutes away, and the spell was broken. Immediately Callie pulled her hand from under his and placed it in her lap, where it couldn't do anything ridiculous like brush his shampoo ad hair out of his face. She drank from her chocolate milkshake, and wished she'd ordered something that would actually help quench her suddenly parched throat.

'Do you ever bring Connor here?'

She looked up, saw the apology in his eyes—or was it regret?—and nodded in gratitude.

'Sure. If we do supper we either do it here, or somewhere close to the hotel. It depends on whether we're working or just meeting up.'

They continued their conversation, steering clear of any topics that might reveal anything personal about each other. And, though she longed to know more, she didn't ask about his family, or the mysterious woman in his past. She didn't think he spoke of it very much, regardless, and she didn't want to be the one he did it with. She ignored her thoughts that screamed the contrary, and instead focused on eating her food.

At the end of their meal, he offered to take her home.

'No, thanks. I'll just get a taxi.'

'That's silly. It isn't that far, and it's unnecessary for you to pay—' He stopped when he saw the look on her face. 'What?'

'I don't want you to take me home,' she said, because the alternative, *I'd want to invite you in if you did*, wasn't appropriate.

'Of course.' He frowned, and stuffed cash inside the bill. 'Can I at least call you that taxi?

She smiled her gratitude at his acceptance. 'Sure.'

He waited with her for the taxi. Since Sakari was only a few kilometres from the sea she could smell it, and feel the chilly breeze it brought even in summer.

She shivered, and he glanced down at her. Without a word he took off his jacket and laid it over her shoulders. The action brought him face-to-face with her, and gently he pulled at the jacket, drawing her in so that she was pressed to his chest. She felt her breathing accelerate at the feel of his body against hers, at the look in his eyes when they rested on her face.

'What is it about you that makes me forget who I am?' he asked, his voice low and husky, and her skin turned to gooseflesh.

'I could ask you the same thing,' she responded, before she even knew what she was saying.

But their words only encouraged whatever was happening between them, she thought. Especially as they stood together, frozen in time, looking at each other. Neither of them moved—not away from each other, nor any closer—and Callie could feel the hesitation, the uncertainty that hung between them. She could also feel the want, the need, that kept them there despite the ambiguity of their feelings.

The longer she stood there, the more pressing her desire to kiss him became, and she moved forward, just a touch, so that their lips were a breath away from each other's. His eyes heated and he leaned down. Callie closed her eyes, lost in anticipation of the kiss...

The sound of a car's horn pierced the air and they jerked apart. She lost her balance, and was sure she would soon be landing on her butt, but a strong arm snaked around her waist and pulled her upright. Again she found herself in Blake's arms, almost exactly as she had been a few moments before, but the magic had passed.

She cleared her throat. 'Thanks for…um…saving me.'

'Of course.' His words were stilted. 'I assume that's your taxi?'

She turned and looked around and saw that the hoot had indeed come from a taxi. She closed her eyes in frustration and then turned back to him.

'Yeah, it is. Thanks again.' She gestured towards the restaurant and felt like an idiot. 'And…um…I hope you feel more confident about the tour for the proposal now, having seen some of the stops.'

He stuffed his hands in his pockets. 'I do. I enjoyed today. I'll see you tomorrow.'

She nodded and smiled, and then awkwardly walked to the taxi, knowing he was still watching her. She lifted her hand as the taxi pulled away, and resisted the urge to look back at him.

'Blake?' Callie pushed open the conference room door and saw him sitting at the head of the table, where she'd found him the first time.

Was that only yesterday? she wondered, and nodded a greeting when he looked up.

'Morning,' Blake said, his tone brisk, and immediately Callie's back went up. 'Grab a seat and we can start talking about the proposal.'

Callie stood for a moment and wondered if this was a joke. There was no familiarity in his tone, no semblance of the man she'd spent the day with.

The man she had nearly kissed.

When he looked up at her expectantly she walked to a seat at the table and felt her temper ignite.

'So, I've gone over your list of places—including the ones we saw yesterday.'

Oh, she thought, so he *did* remember it. 'Yes...?'

'I have some ideas on how to complement the business side of the proposal with the tour. Have a look at these and let me know what you think.'

Callie took the papers he offered her and began to look through them. But somehow she kept reading the same line over and over again.

What was wrong with him? He was treating her as he had after that welcoming event. Cold, brisk, professional. The aloof and unattainable boss. She knew she shouldn't expect more from him—or *anything* from him, for that matter—but she'd hoped that their day yesterday, the things they'd learned about one another, the attraction they'd *both* felt, would have eased things between them. She didn't want her spine to feel like steel from the tension in the room. And yet that was exactly what was happening.

She cleared her throat as she built up the nerve to address it. 'Blake, did I upset you last night?'

He barely acknowledged that she was speaking, but she pushed on.

'When I told you I didn't want you to take me home? Or when we nearly—'

'Callie, I don't need you to explain anything. I just need you to read through the document and tell me your thoughts on it.'

He continued working on his laptop and didn't see her jaw drop. Just as quickly as it had dropped, she closed it again. This wasn't the man she'd spent the day with yesterday, she realised. Now she was dealing with her boss. The one who had made her feel as if she was dishonest and nosy when she'd first met him.

Suddenly all the regrets she'd had about not letting him take her home, about not kissing him, about not telling him more about herself faded away. All the questions she'd wanted to ask him about his mother, his father, the woman he wouldn't talk about, no longer mattered.

She should be thanking him, she thought. He was saving her, really. She didn't have to worry about developing feelings for him. She didn't have to think about opening up to him. She didn't have to open up to her boss. She could be just as brisk and aloof as he was.

'Of course,' she replied, and read through the document, making notes and ignoring the disappointment that filled her.

Blake threw his pen against the door five minutes after Callie had left for the day. It had been a week since their tour together. Seven days of complete torture, five of which she'd spent sitting across from him, answering all his questions politely, only speaking when it had to do with work.

And *he'd* done that. He'd pushed her away with his professionalism. The stupid professionalism that he'd prided himself on before Julia. No, he thought. He'd never been this bad before Julia. She'd made him into this cold person. This person who didn't open up even when he wanted to.

He closed his eyes and leaned back in his chair.

That wasn't completely fair. Julia may have brought it out in him, but he'd made the decision to be cold. Just like now, when he'd decided that after the day they'd spent together—after he'd almost told her too much…after he'd almost kissed her—that Callie was too dangerous to his resolve to stay away from relationships.

So he'd ignored the fact that their day had meant something to him and dealt with her just as he dealt with any other employee. And each time he did, he could sense the animosity growing inside her.

She didn't deserve this, he thought, and loosened the tie which seemed to be strangling him. She didn't deserve to feel as if she had been the only one to want something more than professionalism.

But it had to be this way. Or else, if they started something, he might begin to need her—to want her and want things he'd forgotten about a long time ago. Julia had done a number on him, he knew, but he'd deserved it after the way he'd reacted to her. He'd been attracted to her like no one else before, and she'd had a sweet kid who'd needed a father.

He rubbed his hands over his face and thought about the first time he'd met Brent. He and Julia hadn't been dating very long—perhaps a month—when she'd brought the boy to work with her because her babysitter for the school holidays was sick that day. Brent had been sitting with Julia at the table when Blake had got to the restaurant where they'd planned to have lunch. Blake had known Julia had a son, but hadn't thought too much about it until he'd met the boy.

'I'm glad you two finally get to meet,' she'd said, her arm around her son's chair. 'Brent, this is the man that I've been telling you about.'

The boy had looked up with solemn eyes, and examined him for a long time. Then he'd asked Blake, 'Are you going to be my new daddy?'

It had shocked him, and he'd resisted the urge to laugh nervously. But then he'd looked up into Julia's eyes, seen what he'd wanted to see, and replied, 'Maybe.'

He shook his head and stood now, his body tight from sitting at the table for the entire day. And from the direction of his thoughts. Being around Callie brought up all sorts of emotions inside him, and awakened memories he'd thought he'd put to rest.

Such as the fact that he had wanted to give that boy a family like the one he'd never had.

His mother had done a number on his father as well, and since then he and his father had always focused on their joint interests instead of on family. He'd never had a normal family situation. Just as he had told Callie.

Which was exactly why being professional with her was so important. He couldn't afford to fall for her. She was everything he had tried to stay away from, and he'd already revealed things to her that he didn't even think he'd known about himself.

It was the best decision to distance himself, Blake decided. And he didn't question why it felt so wrong.

CHAPTER SEVEN

'CALLIE, BLAKE NEEDS TO see you in Conference Room A.'

Kate popped her head into Callie's office and then disappeared almost immediately. But not before Callie saw the expression on her face. She recognised that expression. It was the sympathetic one Kate usually wore when Callie told her about a horrible tour she'd been on.

Was Blake annoyed with her? She'd left him a note in the conference room to tell him that she wanted to prepare alone before their first potential investor arrived at ten. As she made her way to the conference room she faced the fact that it was certainly a possibility. He might have wanted to talk to her about the proposal and run through it one last time.

But she hadn't wanted to deal with him that morning, when her nerves had already been tightly coiled. Just being in his presence made her feel so tense that sometimes she felt sick. So this morning, before the most important tour of her life, she'd just wanted a bit of peace.

When she arrived at the room she saw Blake standing with his back facing the door.

'Blake? Kate said you wanted to see me?'

He turned to her, his face calm, though she thought she saw an eyebrow twitch. She took a step towards him and then stopped when she realised she'd mistaken calm for professional. It was the same look he'd had on his face when she'd walked in on him and Connor talking the day all this had started.

'What do you need me for?'

'Both Mr Vercelli and Mr Jung arrived this morning. Apparently Mr Jung had an urgent matter to resolve in South Africa, and so took an earlier flight to Cape Town. Instead of individual proposals, customised for two different potential investors, we're going to have to do them both today.'

Callie felt her stomach churn, and sat down on one of the conference room chairs so her legs didn't give out on her. She closed her eyes and let her mind go through the possibilities. Could they still do two different proposals? No, that wouldn't work. And nor could they make one of the men wait, do it in two shifts, since both proposals included dinner.

'Callie?'

Blake was crouched in front of her when she opened her eyes.

'Are you okay? You're pale.'

He brushed a piece of hair out of her face and her mind, which had been so busy before, blanked. And then she remembered that they had a job to do and nodded.

'I'm fine.' She stood, and he rose with her, and for a moment they were so close she could feel his body heat. 'What does this mean, though?'

'It means we need to work on a new plan that merges the two proposals.' He said it confidently, his voice back to its usual formality, as though this had always been his plan and he hadn't just shown his concern for her.

'And you aren't in the least worried that this might turn out poorly?' she asked, her own fears motivating words that she wouldn't have spoken if it didn't irk her that he had recovered from their contact much faster than she had.

'No, Callie, I'm not. This is what I do.'

He shrugged and walked around her, and she thanked the heavens when her mind started working normally again.

'And, today, this is what *we* do.'

His emphasis stiffened her spine and she realised he wanted her to step up. So she took a moment, searching through the possibilities, looking for some way to maintain the two proposals they'd worked on. She knew both tours like the back of her hand, and before she could consciously think about it she started pulling threads of commonality from each of them.

'Okay…so Mr Vercelli wants to experience the Italian side of Cape Town—family was our angle on that one.' She spoke almost without realising it, needing to hear her ideas out loud to figure out whether they made sense. 'And Mr Jung wants to experience Cape Town culture, which we know is so different from his own Chinese culture.'

She frowned, and then looked up at Blake.

'But isn't family in a place fondly called the Mother City an important part of our culture?'

Blake smiled at her, and she felt the knot in her stomach loosen.

'I'd say so, yes. I think you're on to something.'

She returned his smile. 'So we focus on the common aspect of the two proposals—family. We use tour stops and business details focused on that.'

'Yes, that should work.'

She waited for him to grab his tablet from the table to note things down. But instead he just stood leaning against the table slightly, with a satisfied look on his face.

'You'd already thought about that, hadn't you?' she asked.

'I had. But you needed to get there yourself.'

She shook her head and sat down, not sure if she was relieved that her idea was one he approved of or annoyed that he'd already thought of it and had let her panic for nothing.

'So what's the plan?' she asked in resignation, and listened as he outlined his thoughts, only objecting when she thought she had something valuable to add.

And even though she knew he was good at his job—even though his calm and commanding presence gave her some stability—she still found herself saying the words that mingled with her every thought.

'This *is* going to work, right?'

He looked at her, and something on her face prompted him to sit in the chair opposite her. He placed his hands on her arms and the heat seeped through her jacket right down to her blood.

'This is going to work. And I would know, since I've already seen you in action when you haven't had the time to plan anything.' He squeezed her arms. 'You're good at what you do spontaneously, and you still have some time to prepare now, while Connor is with them. Think about how awesome you're going to be with weeks of preparation and fifteen minutes of practice.' He smiled, and her lips curved in response. 'This is going to work.'

'Thanks,' she said as he stood, and something made her want to offer him the same comfort, even though she knew he didn't need it. 'Blake? I've seen you work. And your passion, your dedication, doesn't come close to anything I've ever seen before. I know you didn't *have* to get new investors, or do as much as you have to save our jobs when the hotel would have probably been more successful if you had downsized.' She shrugged and then continued softly, 'I'm still not sure why you agreed to this, but I'm thankful that you did. We all are.'

He nodded, with a mixture of emotions on his face that were complicated enough that she didn't try to read them.

Instead, she simply said, 'Shall we do this?'

'As you can see, this is the best place to see Cape Town from and look around. Families—tourists and residents alike—all come here to experience the best of the Mother City. This is such an integral part of the family culture of Cape Town—the culture our tourists specifically come for—and now you get to experience it for yourself.'

Blake smiled, though he was sure their two potential investors barely saw it. Not when they'd hung on to Callie's every word from the moment she'd introduced herself in the conference room that morning. She had done so confidently, as if they had always expected Mr Vercelli—who had insisted they call him by his first name, Marco—and Mr Jung to arrive at the same time.

He looked over at the two men who were admiring the view of Cape Town from its signature attraction. Mr Jung caught his eye and nodded, as though silently agreeing that this might be one of the most beautiful places in the world, his grey hair blowing in the wind. He wasn't a man of many words, but he wielded a lot of power.

Blake had his finger in pies that didn't have anything to do with the hotels, and in his previous dealings with Mr Jung he had been fair and open to suggestions. And that meant fertile ground for his expansion plans, he thought, and knew he had to do everything in his power to make sure this proposal was the best it could possibly be.

'At sunset, this experience is even more beautiful.'

Callie smiled at him, acknowledging that these were words she'd said to him once before. Except then it had just been the two of them, and Blake had felt something inside him longing, which was decidedly not the case now.

'I think that would be a…er…wonderful thing, Callie.' Marco's Italian accent was thick, and his words were punctuated by pauses every now and then, but otherwise his English was flawless. 'I would love that.'

'And I would love to bring you up here.'

She smiled again, and Blake knew that part of the reason she was handling these businessmen so seamlessly was because of their appreciation of that smile.

'If you invest, our hotel's connections with the staff here would mean we wouldn't even have to wait in line.'

She smiled again, and Marco burst out laughing. She even coaxed a smile out of Mr Jung.

'You have a firecracker here, Blake,' Marco said. 'I might even steal her for one of my hotels in Italy!'

'You would have to get through me first,' Blake said, and saw Callie's eyes widen. It reminded him of her expression just before they'd almost kissed that night so long ago, when he had pulled her in closer to him...

She bit her lip and he realised that he'd been staring. And that Marco was looking at him with amusement.

He turned his attention back to the Italian man

and smiled. 'Unless you invest, Marco, in which case we can negotiate!'

The boisterous laughter that erupted from Marco made him think that perhaps he hadn't lost face. But he'd nearly lost his composure, he thought, and forced himself to focus.

Clearly the businessmen weren't the only ones captivated by Callie's smile. Her proximity made him say things, do things that he wouldn't otherwise. Even as she stood now, prim and proper in a black dress and red heels, a matching jacket lying over her arms, he wanted her with a need that surpassed even that which he had felt for Julia.

He cleared his throat. 'Now that you've had a chance to see it for yourself, gentlemen, you can understand how the Elegance's proximity to Table Mountain is an asset for the hotel. We arrange for free shuttles on request, to drop and fetch our guests at the location, with the added benefit of guided tours if the guest desires it. We've also negotiated special rates for families with the Table Mountain tourism management, so all our guests will be able to enjoy this experience together.'

He assumed that the nods from both the men

meant they were on board thus far. Now, he thought, to keep going for the next seven hours...

'I think we actually pulled that off,' Callie said as she watched the two businessmen being escorted back to the Elegance from their final stop at the V&A Waterfront, where they'd had dinner.

As soon as they'd been driven away she turned and grinned at Blake.

'We did,' he agreed, and shocked her by picking her up and spinning in a circle.

She laughed, but when he put her down and they stood in each other's arms she felt herself wanting him. She wanted to slide her hands around his waist and pull him close. To celebrate the success of the day. The stars gleaming down on them seemed to encourage her, seemed to tell her that it was the perfect moment to lean forward and kiss him.

But a couple of people nearby whistled at them, and broke her from her trance. She stepped back from him and smiled at their spectators. And when she turned back to Blake he was smiling at her.

'What?' she asked, wondering what the strange look on his face was.

'Nothing,' he responded, and tucked her hair behind her ear.

His hand lingered there, and again Callie found herself wishing that he would just kiss her. Then he took his hand away and stuffed it in his pocket, as though it was being punished.

'We should go and have a celebratory drink.'

'What?' Shock seeped right through to her bones. Based on the last five minutes they'd spent together, the last thing they should be doing was spending time alone with each other.

'I think we should grab a drink to celebrate.'

He took her hand and led her through the throngs of people who were out and about, despite it being a weekday evening.

'And you can actually eat something instead of answering questions while we're at it.'

Before Callie could fully process what was happening they were walking towards the dock. She frowned, knowing that there were very few bars or restaurants on this side of the waterfront. And then she stopped dead when he led her to a boat with two men standing on either side of the steps that led to its entrance.

'What is happening, Blake?'

'We've having drinks. Come on.'

He walked towards the steps, but she didn't budge.

'Callie?'

'I don't think you understand.' Now she did take a step forward. 'This is a boat. They don't just serve drinks on private boats for people who decide that they should celebrate.'

'No, they don't,' he agreed. 'But they *do* serve drinks on boats for people who own them and decide to celebrate.'

She stared at him. 'You *own* this boat?'

'As of two weeks ago—yes. Now, will you come with me?'

Callie followed him purely on instinct. Her mind was too busy thinking about the fact that she was having drinks on a boat with her boss. And that the boat belonged to him. Two weeks ago? That had been after they'd spent the day together...

She still hadn't come to terms with it all when he pulled a seat out for her at a table in the centre of the deck. The edges of the boat were lined with tiny lanterns, which lit the boat with a softer light than the full moon offered from the sky. Champagne chilled in a bucket next to the table, and one of the men who had waited for them to get on the boat now filled their glasses with it. The other still waited at the entrance to the boat, she saw, though he didn't make any move to cast off.

'How did you do this?' She finally looked at Blake, who was wearing a very self-assured grin.

'I called a few people.'

'But when?' she whispered, afraid she would embarrass him. 'We've barely had fifteen minutes since Marco and Mr Jung left.'

'Oh, that.' He was still smiling as if he had just pulled off the world's biggest heist. 'During dinner. I knew today had been successful, and I wanted to do something on a par with what we pulled off. So I made a few calls and here we are.'

'Firstly, I'm pretty sure this *surpasses* what we pulled off. And, secondly, dinner was only about an hour ago.'

'Are you complaining?'

'No, but I feel sorry for these men. How often do they have to do this?'

'I'm not sure about their previous employers, but since they've only worked for me for two weeks this is the first time I've asked them anything. Don't worry—I've made it worth their while. Besides, this is minimal effort since we aren't going anywhere. Now...' he lifted his champagne glass '...shall we toast to what we did today?'

Callie lifted her glass and toasted, but she still couldn't believe she was on a boat. Okay, they weren't sailing anywhere, but privacy after the day they'd had was exactly what she needed. Although she wasn't sure if privacy with Blake was the smartest kind.

'Did you buy this boat after our tour together?'

'I did.'

He didn't offer anything else, and Callie thought perhaps she should be more specific.

'Did you buy this boat *because* of our tour together?'

'Not really—although our time on the boat did give me some fond memories.' He grinned and ran a hand through his hair. 'You're thinking too much about this, Callie. I wanted a boat so that I can have some peace when I need it. That's what you told me, right? To do things that make me happy.' He shrugged when she frowned at him. 'Let's just focus on tonight, okay? I wanted to do something nice for you to say thank you. And well done.'

'Well, you didn't have to. Especially not this.' She gestured around her, though she could see that maybe he was trying to reassure himself more than he was her. Especially after telling her that he'd bought the boat to make himself happy. 'I was just doing my job. And I wouldn't have been able to, I don't think, if it wasn't for you.'

'If you're talking about the fact that these proposals might help to save your job, and all those at the hotel—'

'Actually, no. I'm talking about what you said to me before we left this morning.'

He frowned. 'That you could do it?'

'Yeah.' She laughed a little, feeling silly for telling him this. 'It made me feel like I really *could* do it. And...you know...gave me a boost of confidence.'

He didn't say anything, and she had a sudden burst of doubt. 'I'm sorry, I know that sounds corny—'

'No, it doesn't.'

She felt herself flush when he smiled at her. There was something different about this smile, she thought. It wasn't the cordial you-smiled-at-me-and-I'm-returning-the-gesture type she usually got from him. No, it was a genuine smile that made her remember the completely different Blake she'd first met in the elevator.

The memory awakened other things inside her. Like how much she enjoyed looking at him. The planes of his face, the way his hair fell across his forehead, made butterflies stumble through her stomach.

It's just the atmosphere. Which woman wouldn't have butterflies if a man took her on a boat in the moonlight?

Yeah, she thought, *keep telling yourself that.*

But before she could ponder it further the man who had poured their drinks—she realised now he might very well be a waiter—placed two platters on the table. One held a variety of cheeses and the other a variety of breads and crackers. And, she thought to herself as the waiter described them, she hadn't heard of most of them.

'So you arranged this at dinner? While we were eating?'

He grinned. 'Yes, because even from the starters I could see that you weren't eating very much.'

'Very perceptive,' she said as she spread Camembert on one of the crackers. 'Marco was incredibly interested in some of the sites we took him to. So whenever you were discussing something with Mr Jung he would lean over and ask me about them.' She chewed slowly, contemplating what he had asked her. 'I'm actually not sure if he was asking out of interest or if he was testing me.'

'Well, he definitely seemed impressed. Especially when he told me how much he'd enjoyed the novelty of today's proposal. I don't think he's ever been pitched to for business along with a tour.'

'No wonder you're doing all this. Maybe now would be a good time to ask for a raise.'

He laughed. 'I'll take that under advisement.'

'I'll have Connor put in a good word for me!'

When Blake's face sobered, Callie realised how that might have sounded.

'I was joking, Blake. Connor would never do that.'

'That's not exactly what he told me.'

She frowned, and then remembered the time when he'd told her she would have to pitch to their investors with him. He already seemed to know that her title wasn't a normal one.

'What do you mean?'

Blake drank the rest of his champagne and then asked the waiter to bring him a glass of whisky. She shook her head when he raised his eyebrows and the waiter nodded, presumably concluding that he would only need to bring one glass.

'Connor told me he gave you a job after your parents died.'

'Well,' she said, grasping for something that would make the situation sound better, 'I didn't get paid at first, so it was more of an internship than anything else.'

'He also said that you had been studying towards a degree in anthropology. A degree which, if your human resources file is accurate, you didn't complete.'

Callie opened her mouth and then closed it again. How was she supposed to respond to that?

That it had been an internship was true, but she knew it didn't make sense since she hadn't studied tourism or anything related to what she was now doing. The fact that she hadn't finished her degree made an even stronger case for nepotism, she thought, and cringed when she realised that she was going to have to tell him part of what had really happened.

'Yes, that's true. But Connor was just trying to help me.' She had long since stopped eating, but the food felt like lead in her stomach. 'I...I didn't cope very well with my parents' deaths. So, yes, maybe Connor wasn't being completely professional when he got me the internship. But I've worked incredibly hard for the hotel. And I've built up a good reputation with our tours. I can show you—'

'Callie.'

Blake was looking at her strangely, and she felt her heart stuck in her throat.

'I'm not asking you to defend your job.'

'I know that,' she said, and resisted the urge to shake out her shoulders. 'I just...just thought you should know that Connor has never done anything like that again. It was a one-time thing.'

Blake didn't say anything for a while. The waiter brought his whisky and Blake thanked him. After what seemed like an eternity he drank, put his glass down and settled back into his chair.

'I was there when we hired Connor. Did you know that?'

She shook her head, wondering where he was going with this.

'My dad was still in charge then, and Connor started out as the operations manager of the Cape Town branch. During his interview I remember thinking that he was going to be a good fit for the hotel. He understood our values and seemed just as dedicated to our guests as we were. And then he worked his way up and I had the honour of seeing how much of himself he invested into the job. And the pride he took in the work he did. When I promoted him to regional manager he told me that he would make sure we got out of the mess Landon had made.'

He paused, and bit into a piece of cheese.

'Of course neither of us really knew the extent of the damage Landon had caused. But that's beside the point. What I'm trying to tell you, Callie, is that I was always fairly sure of your brother's character. Only one thing has gone against the opinion I had of him—*your* appointment.'

Callie wished she could stand up and give her restless legs something to do. But she didn't think that would be wise, considering that she was on a boat with men who would probably think she was crazy if she did. Instead she pushed a hand through her hair, resisting the urge to pull at it.

'You know, Blake, sometimes we do things for our family that go against what we believe in.' She cautioned herself against the fury she felt behind her words, but it didn't work. 'I know *your* family wasn't like that, but in mine we did things for one another. Helped each other. Supported each other.'

She rubbed her hands over her face and almost immediately her anger fizzled out.

'I'm sorry. That was uncalled for.'

Blake's face had blanched at her words, but he nodded. 'It was.'

Callie bit her lip, and hated herself for lashing out. 'It's just that Connor saved my life with this job. No, he really did.' Tears pricked at the backs of her eyes but she forced them back. 'My parents' deaths nearly destroyed me.'

There—she'd said it. The words she'd never really said aloud to anyone else. She was afraid to look up, to see the pity she knew would be in his eyes. She didn't want that. It would remind her of how almost everyone had treated her after her parents had died. As if she was something to be pitied.

She looked up at him when she felt his hand gentle on hers, and there was no pity in his eyes. Just compassion. And she felt the coldness that had started to chill her bones thaw.

CHAPTER EIGHT

BLAKE KNEW HE shouldn't have pushed, but he'd wanted to know. He'd needed to. Callie awakened desires in him that had been dormant since… well, since Julia. And even then, he hadn't needed to know her this badly.

Ever since Callie had told him about her parents' deaths Blake had wanted to ask her about it. He wanted to know how she'd handled it, who had been there to support her. The information he had gathered from Connor after she'd mentioned it and the little he had shared with Callie a few moments ago had only made him more curious. Especially since he knew that her specialist job wasn't something that existed in any of the other hotels.

But now, seeing her anguish right in front of him, he felt like an absolute jerk.

'I'm sorry you had go through that,' he said, wishing there was something more he could say.

She slid her hand from beneath his and laid it on her lap. 'I am, too.' She attempted to smile, but her sadness undermined its effect.

'Well, you don't need to talk about it.' He gestured to Rob, the man who had been serving them all night. 'Could you bring some tea for Miss McKenzie, please?' Rob nodded, and Blake turned his attention back to Callie. 'I figure you could use something a little more soothing than champagne.'

'Thanks.' She smiled again, and this time it wasn't quite as sad. And then she took a deep breath and said, 'Blake, I…I want to tell you what happened when my parents died, okay? But only because I need you to understand why Connor did what he did. And then can we pretend this conversation never happened?'

She looked at him with such innocent hope that he nodded, even though he knew that pretending it had never happened would probably—well, never happen.

She angled her head, and didn't meet his eyes as she spoke.

'My parents were on their way home from a weekend away. It was their anniversary, and every year they celebrated by staying at the hotel where they'd had their wedding. They'd been married twenty years.' She cleared her throat. 'A drunk driver overtook when he wasn't supposed to and crashed into them. They died instantly.'

She looked up at him.

'I was nineteen. Old enough to survive.'

But still young enough to need them, he thought, but didn't say it in case it interrupted her.

'My parents meant the world to me. We were incredibly close, and losing them…it felt like I'd lost a piece of myself.'

He reached for her hand again when he saw she was fighting back tears.

'I was incredibly depressed. I couldn't go back to university. I shut my friends out. I shut Connor out. I just felt like I was in this dark room and I was flailing around, trying to find a light.'

She paused when Rob, the waiter, returned with a pot of tea, but barely waited until he'd left before she continued.

'My friends couldn't deal with the morbid person I had become. One by one, each of them disappeared. Until even my best friend—well, I thought she was—couldn't do it any more.'

She lifted her eyes to his, and gave him a sad smile.

'Death is one of those things that you can only truly understand when it affects you. Sure, people are there for you at the funeral, and sometimes a few weeks after. But when you realise that this is your life now—that you have to live without the family who were so integral to your existence— even those people fade away. Because how can they understand that the life you knew no longer exists when theirs is going on as normal? Connor struggled too, but he had his job. Something that gave him purpose. I think that's probably around the time he started climbing the ladder at the El- egance. But when I didn't go back to university I think an alarm went off for him and he realised how lost I was. So he pitched up at my house one morning and forced me to go to work with him.'

She smiled at the memory.

'I hated him for it, but he just told me to start shadowing the concierges. He did that every day for two months. And then one day I realised that I wasn't walking around in a coma any more. I found myself asking questions and engaging with the guests. And that's how the tours came about.'

Blake had known that it would be something like that. He hadn't been lying when he'd told Callie he knew Connor pretty well, and the man he knew would have never given his sister a job just because he could. But the truth was he didn't really care why Connor had done it. He was more interested in Callie, and in the events that had had her starting at the hotel. That now had her desperate to save it. All of a sudden, it made sense to him.

'I wondered why you wanted to save the hotel so badly.' He looked at her and wished he could do something about that wounded expression on her face. 'I knew it was because of Connor. And, of course, your job. But now I understand that the reason behind it is because they saved you. Connor and your job helped you cope with your parents' deaths.'

'Yes,' she said, surprise coating her features, 'that's exactly it.'

He drank the last of his whisky and put the glass down with a little bit of a bang. 'I'm definitely glad I listened to you, then.'

She laughed—a husky sound because of the emotion she had told her story with. 'I'm glad you listened, too. Or I might be out on the streets and not out on a boat.'

Blake grinned, and slowly began to realise that he believed what he'd said. He *was* glad he'd listened to Callie. If he hadn't he would have had to let staff go and face another example of his own poor judgement. He would have had to tell his father what had happened and face his reaction. And all the hard work he had put into building his own legacy—not merely being a part of his father's—would have been for nothing.

As he asked Rob to bring him coffee he realised that Callie's ghosts weren't the only ones that had been stirred that night.

'What's wrong?' Callie asked, holding her breath at the expression on Blake's face.

Emotions she couldn't identify flashed through his eyes, but then he shook his head and smiled at her.

'Nothing. Just thinking that it's been a tiring day.'

And it had been, she thought. Except that *wasn't* what he was thinking. Maybe he was thinking of a way to fire her. Or to fire Connor. She had just admitted that Connor had given her a job—or rather an internship—to help her through her parents' deaths. And even though Connor's intentions might have been good, that didn't matter in the real world. Professionalism mattered. Ethics.

She shouldn't have told him any of it, she thought. She had just been trying to get him to see that she had earned her job. Why did the way it had started out matter? But at the same time she had told him about the worst part of her past. She had opened up to him. Her heart accelerated at the thought. She had done exactly what Connor had encouraged her to do so often. Except she'd done it with her boss. The man who had the power to kick her out of his hotel and make sure she never worked in the hospitality industry again.

She bit her lip and searched Blake's face, hoping she would find the truth of what he was thinking somewhere. What she saw worried her even more.

'Blake…look, I'm sorry if I overstepped. I probably shouldn't have told you any of this.'

'What?' He looked up at her distractedly and whatever he saw must have alerted him to her paranoia. 'Callie, no—I am so glad you told me. I understand.'

His face softened and something made her think that perhaps he wanted to say *I understand you so much better now.*

He laid a hand over hers. 'Thank you for telling me. I know it wasn't easy for you.'

'It wasn't.' The heat from his hand slid through her entire body. 'And if you're not upset with me, that means you're thinking about something that isn't easy for *you.*'

He frowned up at her.

'Come on, Blake. We've spent almost all our time together for the last two weeks. You don't think I know when something's bothering you?'

'Look, it's honestly nothing. I was just thinking that getting investors is probably the best solution for the hotel.'

'And that upsets you?'

'No.' Rob placed coffee in front of him, and Blake waited until he was gone before continuing. 'I was just so set on saving the legacy of the hotel that I would rather have retrenched staff whose livelihood was on the line—as you so nicely reminded me—than think about my father being disappointed in me—'

He stopped abruptly, and Callie realised he hadn't meant to say that. But because he had, things began to fall into place for her. Snippets of their conversation on the day of their tour filled her mind. His relationship with his father. His mother leaving. The legacy. As she put them together she thought she knew what was bothering him.

'There's nothing wrong with wanting to make your father proud,' she said gently.

He shook his head. 'I don't know where that came from.'

She smiled, wondering if he realised how much of a man he was being. 'You were being honest with yourself.'

He angled his head, didn't meet her eyes, and she realised he didn't enjoy being honest with himself. Which, if she knew him well enough to guess, meant that he had halted any thoughts that would continue along those lines.

'Blake, was your dad upset when your mom left?'

He looked up at her in surprise. 'Of course

he was. But I don't see what that has to do with anything.'

Of course you don't.

'So they'd had a good relationship?'

'I don't know.' He shrugged. 'My dad always used to say they were partners—so, yeah, I guess so.'

'Do you know *why* she left?' Callie didn't want to ask, but she knew that the answer would help her put the final piece into place. And help Blake to do the same.

'Callie—'

'Blake, please...' she said, seeing the resistance in his eyes. 'I want to understand.'

Especially because I still feel raw from telling you about my parents.

'My father said she didn't want us any more.'

He clenched his teeth, and Callie resisted the urge to loosen the fist his hand had curled into.

'That she'd left us for someone else.'

She felt her heart break for the little boy who had heard those words. For the man who still suffered from them.

'She disappointed him?'

He drew a ragged breath. 'And me.'

'And now you don't want to disappoint him, or yourself, like she did?'

He didn't answer at first, and then he looked at her. She saw his eyes clear slightly, and resisted the urge to smile at his expression.

'I guess so.'

Now she did smile. 'Should I ask the waiter to warm up your coffee?'

'What?' He was still staring at her in bemusement.

'Your coffee.' She gestured towards it. 'It's probably cold. Actually, so is my tea.' She signalled to the man and asked him to bring them fresh beverages.

'Callie, did you just psychoanalyse me?'

'No,' she said, putting on her most innocent expression. 'I was merely pointing out why it's important to you to make your father proud.'

He stared at her for a moment, and then shook his head with a smile. 'I think you missed your calling in life. You would have had a field day with me when I got married.'

Callie felt her insides freeze. The smile she had on her lips faded and she thought time slowed.

'What did you say?'

Blake was still smiling when he answered her. 'I said you've missed your calling in life.' And then he saw her face, and his eyes widened. 'Callie—'

'You're *married*?'

'No, I'm not. I got divorced a long time ago.'

'Oh…okay,' she said shakily, and wondered why she hadn't thought about it.

He was, after all, an attractive, successful man in his thirties. It shouldn't surprise her that he had been married. Though the divorce was a surprise, she thought, and thanked the waiter—why didn't she know his name yet?—as he placed her tea in front of her.

She went through the motions of making a cup, and remembered the first time they'd met, when Blake had told her that he tried to stay away from women. She'd attributed it to a bad relationship. She'd known there was a mysterious woman. So why hadn't she considered an ex-wife until just now?

'So she was the piece of work we spoke about in that elevator?'

'I don't think we've ever spoken about that.'

'Yeah, we have.' She didn't look up at him, just

kept on staring intently at the milky colour of her tea. She hadn't let it stand for long enough, she thought. 'When you said that you don't put moves on women, that you stay away from them, I told you that whoever had made you feel that way must have been a real piece of work.' She lifted her eyes to his and asked, '*Was* she?'

His face hardened. 'Callie, this isn't any of your business.'

'It isn't.' Suddenly the surprise that she'd experienced only a few moments ago morphed into anger. 'But neither was my parents' deaths yours.'

'That isn't the same thing. You told me about that because you wanted to explain why Connor hired you. And since he hired you into *my* company I had the right to know.'

She quickly realised that the reason she'd told him about her parents' deaths, about how she'd coped and how Connor had saved her—the reason he had just provided—was a lie.

'You and I both know that I wasn't telling you because I work for you,' she said in a measured voice. 'But, since we're talking about it, was what you told me about *your* parents any of my business?'

'No, it wasn't.' His tone mirrored hers, but it was lined with the coldness she was beginning to recognise he used when he spoke to her as her boss.

'And all of this—' she gestured around her '—is what you do for someone you don't want in your business?'

'I was just saying thank you to an employee for a job well done.'

She stared at him, wondering if he really believed the nonsense that was coming out of his mouth. She gave him a moment to come to his senses, to salvage the progress they'd made, but he said nothing.

'Well, in that case remind me to compare notes with Connor about employee rewards.'

She gathered her things and walked towards the man who had stood silently at the entrance of the boat since they arrived.

'Would you please help me off this boat?' she asked him, and realised that she didn't know *his* name either.

He smiled kindly at her. 'Of course, ma'am.'

Before she climbed the steep stairs up to the dock, she turned back to Blake. 'She must have done something really awful to you, Blake, for you to push away something that could have...' She faltered, but then said it anyway. 'That could have *been* something. But don't worry. The next time I see you we can pretend nothing that happened this evening actually happened. Just to ensure that we stay out of one another's business.'

He didn't move in his seat—in fact he hadn't even turned while she'd been talking to him. She shut down all the hurt flooding through her and nodded at the man who was waiting to help her.

She murmured a thank you when she reached the top, and then she was walking as fast and as far from the boat—from Blake—as she could.

CHAPTER NINE

CALLIE SIGHED AS she stared at the clock on her desk. It was almost eleven. She had been back at the hotel for almost an hour now, after taking a taxi, and she'd spent that hour clearing her office of the mess she'd made after hastily preparing for their unexpected double proposal.

She was waiting for Blake to arrive and return to his house, so that she didn't bump into him when she popped into her brother's office to give him an update. Connor had said that he'd wait for her to return, and though she knew it wasn't nice of her to make him wait even longer she didn't want to deal with Blake until she'd had a good night's rest.

Or at least that was what she was telling herself.

She sighed and paged through the file she kept on the proposals. So many things had happened that day—that evening. And the evening's events made her want to throw the file in her hand at the door. When Blake had swooped her up into his arms after they'd finished the proposal and taken her to celebrate on his boat—a *boat*—she'd almost laughed at how unbelievable it was. Now she thought that it wasn't as unbelievable as Blake's claim that he was just 'rewarding an employee' by taking her there.

After the things they had shared with one another, after the romance of the evening—and, yes, she acknowledged, to her the whole boat event *had* been heartbreakingly romantic—the fact that he could claim she was just an employee to him hurt. After she had bared her soul to him—and she gritted her teeth at that—how could he callously say such a thing? All because he didn't want to talk about his stupid marriage.

It hurt her more than she wanted to admit that he wouldn't talk to her. Sure, he had told her about his parents' split, and he had been open—however reluctantly—to her conclusion about his subsequent relationship with his father. But then he'd completely shut down when she'd asked him about his ex-wife, going right back to being the stubborn boss she knew and intensely disliked. The one she would never have considered telling about her parents' deaths and how it had broken her.

This was the reason she didn't open up to people, she thought as she began to gather her things. People let you down. One day you had them around you, and you thought that you wouldn't ever feel alone, and the next day they were gone. It didn't matter *why* they left—those reasons always changed—the leaving was the one thing that was always consistent.

So she should be glad that this had happened. Blake was saving her so much heartache by pushing her away. And she would listen to *herself* in the future, not to Connor or any of her colleagues, who insisted that she should open up to people. That she should date.

It was just a waste of time, she thought, and locked her door. Especially if the person she opened up to wasn't ready to do so themselves.

As she made her way to the exit of the hotel she saw that her brother's office door was slightly ajar. Guilt crept in as she remembered that she was supposed to give him an update, and she sighed and detoured to his office. Subconsciously she was hoping that he had already gone home, and she could send him a message when she got home with a quick summary. But he never left his door open after he'd left for the day, so she resigned herself to having to tell him how the day had gone.

It was dark when she peered into the office, with only the city's lights shining through an open window illuminating the room. When her eyes adjusted she saw the outline of a figure in Connor's chair. Her heart thudded and she rushed to his side.

'Connor, are you okay?'

Only when she knelt beside him did she realise that it was Blake, not Connor, sitting at her brother's desk.

'Oh, I'm sorry—I thought you were Connor.' She rose awkwardly to her feet and wished she hadn't let the guilt of responsibility lead her into the lion's den.

'I got that,' he said dryly, and his voice was lined with something she couldn't place her finger on. But she knew it was dangerous.

'I just wanted to fill him in on today.' She eyed the door she had shut when she'd thought something was wrong with her brother, desperately wishing she had left it open.

'I did that. He left a few minutes ago.'

'Oh, okay…' Why was her voice so shaky? 'I'll go, then.'

'No.'

She exhaled sharply. 'What do you want, Blake?'

'I want to apologise.'

'For what?'

'For being a jerk earlier.'

A part of her wanted to brush it off, to tell him that it didn't matter. But she couldn't because…*it did*. It mattered. Everything she had told herself earlier about it being for the best faded somewhere into the background of her mind as she realised this. But she didn't respond to him.

With her eyes fully adjusted, she could see that he no longer had his tie on, and the first few buttons of his shirt were undone. She swallowed, all thought leaving her mind as she noticed that his neck was bare, ready to be kissed. She shook her head and shifted her eyes to his face. It was as gorgeous as it had been the first time she'd admired it, but the danger she had sensed from him earlier was clearly outlined there.

Somewhere at the back of her mind a voice was shouting that she should leave before she had the chance to find out what that danger meant for her. But she didn't move, not until Blake stood, and then she took a step back, bumping into Connor's bookcase. It shuddered, barely moving, but it knocked some of the breath from her.

'I...I can't do this with you, Blake.'

'Do what?'

He was a few feet away from her now. She could smell him, and the sexy scent nearly sent her to her knees. She was suddenly incredibly grateful for the bookcase behind her that held her steady.

'Whatever you have in—'

Her words were cut off as he walked slowly towards her. Her heart rate—which was never really normal around him—kicked up even higher.

'What are you doing?' she asked breathily when there was barely any space between them.

'I'm apologising,' he said, and placed his hands on either side of her.

'It's okay. It's fine.'

She didn't care that she hadn't been ready to accept his apology a few minutes ago.

'Good. But now I'm saying sorry in advance… for doing this.'

And he kissed her.

His lips were soft on hers, and she could barely breathe from the electricity that the contact sparked. She was aware of every part of him—of his hands that were no longer braced beside her but had moved to her waist. Heat seeped through her clothing where he touched her, but it was nothing compared to the inferno of their kiss. He had deepened it, and as though she was outside of her body she heard herself moan.

Her hands slid through his hair and she loved the feel of it through her fingers. Before she knew it he'd pressed her against the bookcase, so that her body was aligned with his. She shuddered at the feel of him against her, and moaned again when he trailed kisses down her neck. She pulled at his shirt and then, with frustration, when she couldn't find his skin fumbled with his buttons. Just as she'd thought, muscles rippled across his chest when the shirt was finally opened and she greedily took them in.

And then froze when his hand slid up her thigh and settled at the base of her underwear.

'Blake…' she rasped, her breath still caught by their passion, 'Blake, we can't.'

His lips stilled at her collarbone, and she could hear that he was just as affected by what was happening between them. He lifted his head and looked at her, and something on her face had him nodding and moving back. She stayed where she was, afraid that her legs wouldn't work if she tried to move.

In the shadowed light from the window he looked amazing, his shirt undone and his abs ripped, just as she'd felt them a few moments before. She wished she could do this, she thought as she took him in. She wished that she hadn't stopped and that they could let their desires control them. But that would only get her more of the hurt she already felt when she was with him.

'I forgive you. For this,' she said breathlessly. 'But I can't do this with you.'

She straightened her dress, picked up the handbag and jacket that she had thrown across the room in her haste to get to her brother. And then she took the minute she needed to organise her thoughts.

'You may have convinced yourself that taking me out on your father's boat was an employee benefit for a job well done, but you can't claim that *this*—' she gestured between them '—is how employees and their employers behave with one another.'

'You're right, it isn't.'

She hadn't noticed that he'd fastened his buttons again. A faint wave a disappointment threaded through her.

'Callie, I meant it when I said I was sorry about earlier.' He braced himself against Connor's desk. 'You didn't deserve that.'

'No, I *did*,' she said, and ignored the surprise on his face. 'I deserved it for believing that letting someone in would do me any good.'

He looked up at her, and something had him moving towards her.

'No—stop.' She held up a hand. 'We've already let this go too far.' She sighed, wishing she could pull her hair out. Anything that would make her feel better about what she was going to say. 'Blake, your ex-wife clearly hurt you. And you'll never really let me in because of that. So, for both of our sakes, I think we should just pretend this never happened.'

'The kiss?' he asked, stuffing his hands into his pockets.

'Everything. Every single thing that's happened between us that shouldn't have happened between a boss and an employee.'

He didn't say anything, and she took that as agreement.

But as she left the office her heart ached at the thought of forgetting what they'd shared.

CHAPTER TEN

'I THINK WE *should just pretend this never happened.'*

Blake welcomed the cold water on his heated and fatigued body. He knew that at some point hot water would be needed to soothe his screaming muscles, but for now the cold took away the pain his two-hour gym session had yielded.

'I think we should just pretend this never happened.'

What it failed to do was wash away the memories of the previous evening. The memories of him acting completely out of character.

Completely out of control.

He'd tossed and turned the entire night, so despite the incredibly long day he'd had, and despite how tired he'd been, he hadn't been able to get a wink of sleep. Which was why he had instead, at four in the morning, made use of his home gym.

He adjusted the water when he felt the cold

down to his bones, and closed his eyes as heat pounded against his body. He had probably pushed himself too far, he thought. And he knew he would pay for it the entire day. Hell, probably for the entire week. But it had kept his thoughts off the mess he had made. For a few hours, at least, he thought, when his mind yet again looped back to the single thing he couldn't stop thinking about.

'I think we should just pretend this never happened.'

He wished he could. He wished he could pretend he hadn't spent the day watching her work. He wished he hadn't noticed how well she had done—how she had taken an unimaginable scenario and turned it into what he was almost certain would be a victory for Elegance. More than anything, he wished he hadn't given in to the impulse of taking her onto his boat.

Yet that wasn't the reason why her words had haunted him from the moment she'd said them. Because, as much as he wished he could pretend everything that had happened between them *hadn't* happened, he couldn't—for one simple reason:

He didn't want to.

He turned the water off and towelled himself dry. He knew the moment Callie had started asking him about his mother that her line of questioning wouldn't be easy for him. He didn't talk about his mother to anyone—he hadn't even mentioned her to Julia—and yet he'd told Callie about her the day they'd had supper after their tour. When he had barely known her.

He had convinced himself that it had just been to comfort Callie, after he'd figured out that her parents had died—especially since she hadn't offered the information freely. But it hadn't taken him long to realise that it had also been because he'd felt comfortable with her. And, if he was honest with himself, that was part of the reason he had insisted on maintaining a professional relationship with her.

If he was comfortable enough to share his most hidden memory with her, it wouldn't take long before she lodged herself in his heart. And then she would be able to hurt him. And if his instincts weren't wrong—as they'd been before—and she'd fallen for him, he'd be able to hurt her, too.

As he began dressing for work he thought about his mother for the first time in years. She *had* disappointed him.

He had watched her pack her bags into the car, and then she'd knelt in front of him and said, 'I'm sorry, Blake. I hope one day you can understand that I couldn't do this. This life was never for me.'

She'd kissed him on the forehead and driven away, and he had watched the car fade into the distance.

He couldn't remember feeling more helpless— or more heartbroken—than at that moment when he was eleven and his mother had left. He didn't know if it mattered to him now that it had been the last time he had seen her or the last time he had known some semblance of a normal family life. But what he *did* know was that he had vowed he would never feel that way again. He didn't ever want to feel as if he didn't have control or to feel heartbroken again. Most of all, he had assured himself that if he were ever a father he would never let his child feel the way he had. He would make sure that *his* child had the family he'd never had.

Something clicked in his head and he realised

that Julia had made him feel all those things—
had forced him to break all those promises he had
made to himself such a long time ago. And the
worst thing was that now he was terrified Brent
would be feeling the same way he had—helpless
and disappointed.

The mess of his mother, Julia and Callie swirled
through his head, and he began to think about his
relationship with Julia in a way he'd never considered before. To think of why he'd reacted the way
he'd reacted to her, why their relationship had
broken down so completely. And though there
were many layers to it—most of which seemed
hazy to him at the moment—one layer suddenly
became incredibly clear.

Blake closed his eyes and resisted knocking his
head against the wall. And he thought one thing
repeatedly—that he was a fool.

Callie got into work early that morning, not bothering with breakfast at home because she knew
she could sneak into the hotel kitchen and grab
some of the food that would be warm and ready
for the breakfast buffet in half an hour.

After doing just that, she unlocked her office

and thanked the office angels who had helped her clear her desk the previous night. Because now she could set her breakfast and her coffee on a desk that she could actually see, instead of on a pile of papers she hoped weren't important.

She sighed as she bit into a warm slice of toast, and moaned when it was accompanied by the coffee boost she so desperately needed. She hadn't slept very well, her mind muddled with thoughts, and at about three in the morning she'd forced herself to stop thinking about the events that had caused the ache in her heart and instead focused on business. She knew the proposal the previous day had gone well, but she wanted to kick it up a notch. At five a.m. she'd had a fully drafted email about what she thought would do just that. Now she just had to find the courage to hit 'send'.

She took her time eating her breakfast, and then read through the email a couple more times. When she couldn't procrastinate any longer she sent the email to Blake, and copied Connor in just in case. She hadn't spoken to him about the proposal, but he'd sent her a message congratulating her. Which she'd only read after midnight, since she had been too busy kissing her boss and dealing with the resulting anguish to switch on her phone before then.

It was barely ten minutes later when she received a response, and she held her breath as she opened it.

Come and see me.

That was it? Nothing about the perfectly outlined event she had just sent him the plan for?

She bit back her disappointment and pulled out her compact mirror to make sure she didn't have breakfast crumbs on her face. She gave herself a pep talk on her way to the conference room and told herself she was as prepared as she would ever be before seeing her boss, with whom she had so hungrily made out the night before. An image of him with an open shirt standing in the moonlight flashed through her mind, but she forced it away.

She was a professional. She could do this.

But her resolve nearly faltered when she saw him. He looked nothing like the dishevelled man she'd left in her brother's office the night before. His hair was slicked back and his suit was pressed. Worst of all, his face was expressionless when he looked up at her.

'Morning, Callie. I just got your email.'

'Yes, I know.' She forced herself to match his demeanour. She was the one who had wanted him to be like this. Except now it didn't seem to be what she wanted at all.

'So…what do you think?'

He ran a hand through his hair and just like that the neat style collapsed as a piece fell over his forehead. He didn't seem to notice, but she did, and she wanted to walk over and fix it for him. And then she could sit on his lap…and then they could continue where they'd left off last night…

She shook her head. Where had *that* come from? She had been so sure that she had made herself immune to him. She'd forced herself to replay every moment of the previous evening and repeated all those words that had hurt her so that she could strengthen her resolve. And then she had forced herself to forget the way his hands had felt on her body, the way he'd kissed like Cupid himself.

She had even dressed the part—loose white linen pants and a cream waterfall jersey that hid the curves of her body effectively. And then she had resolved never to think about him and what he did to her body, to her heart, again. She had focused on her work and come up with a pretty decent idea, even if she said so herself. Now she was just waiting for him to acknowledge it.

'It's a good idea. A really good one.' He tilted his head. 'A gala event for all our potential investors would do wonders for their interest in the hotel. Especially if they're introduced to the competition. I just don't know how you'll be able to pull it off in seven days. Maybe we should push it back?'

'Timing is important.' The words were so formal that she resisted the urge to roll her eyes at herself. 'We should hold the event when the proposals are still fresh in the investors' minds and before the negotiations start, so it can help influence their decisions. That means next Friday is our best bet.'

She sighed when he didn't respond.

'It's just an idea,' she said. 'But I think that if we do this we'll have an opportunity to show the investors the possibility of much larger events in the hotel. So far we've only done corporate events, but if we started adding birthdays, anniversaries, weddings, I think it would be a source of revenue for the hotel that will increase profits immensely.'

'Yes, I saw all that in your email. But how?' Blake stood now, and leaned against the table as he had so many times in the weeks they'd worked together. 'How are we going to pull off the best event the hotel has ever given in a week?'

She faltered. 'We *could* do it. We've racked up favours from all kinds of vendors and services, and I know a lot of them would be grateful for the opportunity to—'

'How long did it take you to organise my welcome event?'

'I didn't organise that. Connor did, mostly.'

'How long did it take Connor to organise the event?'

She bit her lip, and didn't answer him immediately.

'Callie, how long did it take for Connor to organise the event?'

'Fourteen weeks.'

He raised his eyebrows. *'Fourteen?* And you want to throw an event bigger than that in one week? In addition to working on the proposals we'll be doing for four of those seven days?'

She locked her jaw and looked at him. 'Yes.'

'I don't think—'

'Forget it—it's fine.' She turned away.

'Callie, wait,' he said, before she could leave. 'I was going to say I don't think you can do it alone. We'll have to get everyone involved. We need to call in all our favours, with every vendor and every service provider, and make this happen. Because we *can* do it. Together.'

Suddenly Callie was transported back to the previous day, when similar words had made her feel more valued than she ever had before. And she cursed him for still having the ability to make her feel that way.

'Okay, great.'

He smiled at her, though there was something behind it that she hadn't seen before. 'So let's get to it. There's a lot of work to be done.'

Her heart stopped. '*You're* going to help with this?'

He nodded. 'That's generally what's meant by "together".'

'I just thought you meant all the staff.'

'Oh, everyone will help. But you and I will be running it.' He sat down and started typing on his laptop. 'We seem to work well together.'

She stared at him, wondering who had kidnapped the surly boss she'd worked with before and replaced him with this cordial man in front of her.

'Yeah, apparently we do.'

CHAPTER ELEVEN

'ARE YOU READY to go?'

Blake stood in the doorway of her office and she nodded, scribbling a note to remind herself to check when the lights for the gala event would arrive for set-up.

'Let's do this.' She grabbed her handbag and locked up, following him to the front of the hotel. 'I think I might actually be looking forward to this.'

He laughed and nodded his thanks when John pulled the car in front of them. 'It's food—what's not to look forward to?'

How about the fact that we have to do this together?

But she smiled in response, clinging to the truce that had settled between them over the last few days. The proposals were going well, and now, since the German investor they had seen today had had to attend another meeting in the afternoon, they had some more time to work on the gala event.

Blake had arranged that they do a tasting to ensure the catering for the event was good, and she had resigned herself to the fact that she had to go. Eating together—even professionally—seemed dangerously close to a date, but Callie had agreed because she didn't want to rock the boat between her and Blake. She almost rolled her eyes at the description—why did it need to be a *boat*?—but then remembered that Blake always seemed to be watching her recently. And she didn't want to invite any questions she wasn't willing to answer.

'We never really spoke about how you chose this restaurant,' she said once they were in the car, hoping to stop her annoying train of thought.

'This is one of the rare restaurants I've actually been to in Cape Town.'

She looked at him in surprise. 'Really?'

'Yes.' He glanced over at her, but his expression was closed. 'My father has been friends with the owner since before I was born. When we did go out together, it was generally there.'

She frowned. 'Then why are we doing a tasting, if you already know how the food tastes?'

'For several reasons. One being that they've recently hired a new chef. He came with new menus, and I haven't had a chance to taste anything on them yet. Another is that I need you to make sure I've made a decent choice and not just gone with something I know because I trust that the catering will be reliable.'

It made sense, she thought, though she wished he might have said, *Oh, I see your point—we can just skip this.*

'There's a lot to be said for reliability,' she said. 'The last thing we want on Friday is to worry that the food won't be good or won't arrive when it should.'

'Which is why I hope you'll give this place the stamp of approval.'

Callie didn't answer, instead looking out of the window at the hills they passed. She didn't come to this side of Cape Town very often, she thought, as the hills become vineyards. It was a popular venue for large events—weddings, especially—and many of the vineyards offered wine-tastings. Though she had recommended it as a weekend activity for her guests, she had never considered including it on her tours since she knew they would always be battling traffic to get back to the hotel in the afternoons. And, more importantly, she didn't want to deal with tipsy guests and the potential problems they brought.

As Blake turned on to a gravel road that slowly inclined Callie looked up to the top and saw a building made mostly of glass. It was beautifully designed, with curves that spoke of specialised techniques and artistry even to an amateur eye like hers.

'Is that it?' she breathed, but didn't need an answer when Blake pulled into the car park. 'It's *amazing*.'

'It is,' he agreed. 'And the inside is even better.'

He guided her into the restaurant, where they were greeted politely, and while Blake spoke to the maître d' Callie looked around and was forced to agree with Blake about the interior design. Wooden tiles swept across the floor and chandeliers hung from the roof. The glass exterior meant that the restaurant's patrons were treated to a spectacular view of the winelands and, from their position at the top of the hill, some of the city as well.

They were led up spiralling stairs, from where Callie could appreciate the decor of the restaurant even more. It was definitely an upper-class restaurant, but the subtle touches of warmth—like the soft yellow and white table settings—made her think that the owners wanted to avoid the alienating effect more expensive restaurants often had.

When they finally stopped climbing she was out of breath, and she looked around, realising that they had climbed to the top of the building while she had been distracted by aesthetics. And then the maître d' led them through a door and she lost her breath altogether.

'Blake...' she said, but couldn't even continue as she took in the beauty of their location.

She was standing on the rooftop of the restaurant, overlooking the view she had thought so spectacular only a few moments ago. Except now she felt that description had been overzealous, since what she was looking at from here was better than the view through the glass walls.

Blake smiled at her reaction and led her to a

table at the edge of the rooftop, from where she could see everything merely by turning her head to the left.

'How did you arrange this?' she asked, when they were seated and the maître d' had been replaced by a perky waitress.

'Connections,' he said, and shrugged as though sitting on the roof of a restaurant was normal. 'I take it you like it?'

'I really do.'

'So do I,' he said, and looked out to the view. There was a slight breeze that helped lessen the effect of the summer sun and rustled through Blake's hair like leaves during the autumn. 'I don't think I will ever get tired of this.'

She had been wrong, she realised. Even though getting them to the rooftop might have been easy for her boss, the experience wasn't lost on him. That loosened something inside her—something that had stuck the night she had told him to forget everything that had happened between them. The fact that something so simple, something so small, could make her heart ache for him again told her she was in trouble.

So she pulled back, forced herself to act professionally. She made the right sounds when the food was served, agreeing on some dishes, asking for variations on others. She made polite conversation with Blake about the weather, about work, about the event preparations that were coming along nicely. She had almost congratulated herself on surviving when the waitress brought out dessert.

'We've prepared a variety of dishes for you to taste,' said the pretty blonde, who had been incredibly helpful throughout the tasting.

Callie wondered if she had been warned about who she would be dealing with.

'Chocolate mousse, strawberry cheesecake with berry coulis, pecan pie, and a cream cheese and carrot cake trifle.' She pointed at the individual dishes, which were lined up on a long plate. 'You can choose three of these desserts to be served at your event. Please do let me know if you have any questions.'

She smiled brightly at them and then moved to join her colleagues.

Callie frowned as she looked at the plate in front of them, and her stomach dropped when she realised that the waitress wouldn't be bringing out a second. And then she saw the spoons on the table—two of them—and mentally kicked herself for thinking that the restaurant must be encouraging romantic dessert-sharing.

'I suppose we start at each end and move in?' she said, hoping to sound logical about it.

His lips twitched. 'Yes, let's do that.'

She frowned slightly, but chose to ignore him, and instead took a bite from the chocolate mousse. She closed her eyes as it melted in her mouth. She had never tasted anything like it, she thought, and greedily dipped her spoon into the small dish for another bite.

But as she lifted it to her mouth she realised Blake was watching her, and she felt heat flush through her body when she saw the desire in his eyes.

She put the spoon down slowly and said huskily, 'I'm sorry, I suppose I'm being selfish by taking another bite.'

She cringed at her words, knowing full well it wasn't selfishness that had caused her to pause.

He didn't respond, but reached over and took the spoon from her plate instead. 'I don't mind you being selfish,' he said, and lifted the spoon to her mouth.

She opened it on a reflex, though her eyes never left his, and felt a thrill work its way through her body. The mousse melted in her mouth, just as it had the first time, but she didn't taste it now. No, she was remembering the way *he* had tasted when they'd kissed, the way his eyes had heated just as they did now, the electricity that had sparked between them.

The sun was setting behind him, and it cast a glow over them that made everything seem a little surreal—as if they were in a romantic film and about to shoot the perfect ending. She wished it were that which made Blake look like a movie star, but she knew that Blake's looks were not an illusion. Her handsome, gorgeous boss was all too real, and with each moment she spent with him she wanted him to become a part of her reality. She wanted that heat, that electricity, his taste to be hers.

And, even though it couldn't be, for once she didn't fight showing how much she wanted it.

His eyes darkened at what he saw in hers and he placed the spoon down on her plate again and leaned over to kiss her. She felt it right down to her toes…the slow simmer of passion although his lips were only lightly pressed against hers. The taste she had longed for only a few moments earlier was sweeter than the dessert she had just eaten, and it wiped away the memory of it.

She wanted to deepen the kiss, to take more, but the sane, rational part of her brain—the part that was half frozen by his kiss—reminded her that they were in a public place and she pulled back, feeling embarrassed and needy from what she knew had only been a brief kiss.

She reached for her glass of water at almost exactly the same time he did and she drank, grateful that the glass hid the smile that crept onto her face for one silly moment.

He cleared his throat. 'I can tell why you wanted another taste of that.'

She looked up at him in surprise, and bit her lip to stop the bubble of laughter that sat in her throat. But nothing was funny about this, she realised, and the thought banished her lingering amusement.

So she just smiled at him politely, and said, 'We should probably finish the tasting and get back to the hotel. There are a couple more things I need to do before tomorrow.'

And just like that the mood between them shifted.

'Are you done for the day?'

It was like déjà vu, Callie thought as she looked up to see Blake at her office door. It was only a few hours since she'd last seen him there, before they'd gone for the tasting. *Before they'd tasted each other.* She shook her head at the thought, resenting her mind for reminding her of the part of their afternoon that she really wished she could forget.

'Yeah, just about. Why?' She looked down at the papers in front of her, taking care not to look him in the eye.

'Great. Connor's asked me to take you home. He said something about your car breaking down yesterday?'

She was going to kill Connor. 'Yeah, it did. But he said *he* would drop me at home.'

'Something came up.'

Blake didn't seem nearly as concerned as she did about spending time alone together in a car.

Even after the tension that had mounted between them on their way back to the hotel. And the awkward parting they'd shared when they'd arrived.

'It's fine. I'll call a taxi.'

Blake placed a hand on her own, which was reaching for her phone. 'Callie, I'll take you. I don't mind.'

'It's really okay, Blake. I don't want to put you out.'

'This is the second time you've said no to my offer of taking you home.'

She looked at him in surprise when his words were spoken in a terse voice.

'*Why* won't you accept my help?'

'Because you're my boss,' she said, grasping at the one thing that she could cling to. The very external thing that she held on to instead of admitting the real reasons she was pushing him away. 'It isn't appropriate.'

'Can we both stop pretending that's still a factor here?'

'Excuse me?'

'It's the card you pull out every time you want to put distance between us, Callie. We both do.'

She stared at him as he walked into her office and closed the door.

'I know I messed things up between us that night on the boat. I used our professional relationship as an excuse because I was scared. We were getting too close...and my judgement has failed me before.'

He didn't look up at her, but for some reason she could tell his expression would be tortured.

'My ex-wife was an employee. And marrying her was probably the worst decision I've made in my life.'

He lifted his eyes, and she could see that she'd been right. The look on his face tore her heart into two.

'I just don't know if I can trust my judgement any more.'

She could see that the admission had taken a lot from him. And she wished that she could take away the pain that had come with it.

Instead, she bit her lip and said softly, 'I *do* use our professional relationship as an excuse.' She played with a stray thread at the bottom of her jersey. 'To distance myself from you—yes. And because...' She sighed, and gave up on the resistance every part of her screamed out when it came to him. 'Because I don't want to have feelings for you. I don't want to open up to you and have you shut me out again.'

Or, worse, have you leave.

But she couldn't bring herself to say it.

'Do you...? Have feelings for me?'

She shouldn't have said anything, she thought immediately, and then saw the sincerity in his eyes. *Trust me*, they seemed to say, and she spoke as honestly as she could.

'I don't know, Blake. I haven't given myself the chance to entertain even the possibility.'

He nodded. 'And if I promise to...to be open with you, too. Would you entertain the possibility then?'

Her heart accelerated. 'Maybe.'

'Okay.' He held a hand out to her. 'Can I take you home?'

She laughed, and nodded. 'I guess so. I just need to put my shoes on.'

She slipped her left shoe on her foot, and was about to do the same for her right when Blake knelt in front of her.

'Let me.'

He took the shoe from her hand and fitted it onto her right foot. For one ridiculous moment Callie felt as if she was in a fairy tale. Her Prince Charming was kneeling in front of her, fitting onto her foot the shoe that would make her his princess.

But then he looked at her, and all fairy-tale notions fled from her head. There was a heat in his gaze that made her burn from the place where his hand still lay on her foot right up to the hair follicles on her head. For a moment she wondered what would happen if she pinned him against the wall and continued where they had left off a few nights ago...

She shook her head and he smiled at her. But his smile was a wicked one, as though he knew exactly what her mind had jumped to as he'd slipped her shoe on.

He straightened and held out a hand to her. 'Shall we?'

She exhaled shakily and took his hand. 'Yes.'

CHAPTER TWELVE

BLAKE OPENED THE car door for Callie and felt his body tighten when she brushed past him to get in. He supposed he hadn't recovered from their interactions earlier today. That kiss at the restaurant… Whatever it was that had happened in her office…

He didn't know what had possessed him to put her shoe on for her, but he was glad that he had. If he hadn't he wouldn't have seen the way her eyes had sparked with a desire that matched his. She might not know if she had feelings for him, but she definitely wanted him. And that meant they were on the same page.

He watched as she typed her address into the GPS on his dashboard, and when the voice gave him his first direction he followed it. He glanced over at her, and frowned when he saw that her arms were crossed.

'Are you okay?'

'I think so.' She didn't look at him.

'What's on your mind?'

'Nothing,' she said, almost immediately, and then she sighed. 'Everything. I'm just not used to this.'

'To...us?'

She ran a hand through her hair. 'To any of it. This is all new territory for me. Worrying about work. About whatever's going on between the two of us. I don't know—I guess I just feel... *raw.*'

Blake forced himself to keep focusing on the road, even though he wanted to pull over and hold her in his arms. He wanted to comfort her, to tell her that everything was going to be okay. Instead he settled for saying the one thing he thought she might need to hear right now.

'You're not alone, Callie.'

He took a right and didn't look at her, even though he knew her eyes were on him.

'I worry about what's going on between us, too. But you don't have to worry about work, okay? Everything is going to be fine.'

He wanted to ask her if he'd made her feel worse—about her worries over them, about the things she had just told him—but he forced himself to wait. She was opening up to him again and he wanted to earn it. So he just said it again.

'You're not alone.'

The rest of their trip was quiet. Blake didn't know what she was thinking about, but her hands now lay on her lap, and he took it as a sign that maybe she didn't feel so vulnerable any more. He wanted to kick himself for making her feel that way in the first place, but there was nothing he could do about the past. When he'd realised he'd made a mistake about Callie—when he'd realised that the failure of his relationship with Julia had had very little to do with them working together—he had wanted to call her immediately and tell her that he was sorry, that he wanted to make it up to her.

But his words wouldn't have meant anything at that point, he had reasoned, and so instead he'd tried to show her through his actions. He'd made an effort not to keep up the act of being the boss she expected—the hard, cold act he had clung to in order to keep his professionalism with her. Instead he'd acted as he did with every other employee. Well, perhaps not *exactly* the same way, but he figured she'd earned some preferential treatment since her standard of work was higher than most he'd encountered.

He'd also enjoyed the way her eyes widened every time he engaged with her without the cold formality that had coloured his interactions with her before.

When his GPS announced that their destination was on the left, Blake pulled up in front of a light-coloured house with a rush of flowers planted in flower beds along the pathway.

'I'm not sure who to compliment on your garden. You for choosing the flowers, or your gardener for planting them.'

She laughed and unlocked the door. 'Both, I suppose. Thank you. I'll pass the message on to Ernesto.'

He frowned. 'Your gardener's name is *Ernesto*?'

'Yes. He's from Italy. What are the chances of finding a young, attractive male from another country to do your garden for you?'

He couldn't quite keep his face neutral when he thought about it, and she took one look at him before bursting out into laughter.

'I'm just kidding, Blake. My gardener is a lovely man in his fifties called George.'

Her eyes twinkled, and he felt himself relax. And then she gestured to the door.

'Do you want to come inside?'

He barely took a second before saying, 'Sure.'

Her house was spacious, filled with light and bright flowers from her garden. The open plan meant that the lounge, dining room and kitchen led from one room to the other, and all the furniture complemented the warm and rustic theme of her house.

'Did you do the interior of the house?' he asked, walking past a shelf that held pictures of the McKenzie family.

His eyes were drawn to a picture of Callie and Connor, standing next to a woman and a man who looked so much like them he thought that if he'd met them on the street he would have recognised them as Connor and Callie's parents. They looked so happy, he thought, and his heart broke for reasons he couldn't describe. Somehow it made him think of his own family, and the fact that Callie wouldn't ever see a picture like this anywhere in his place.

'Some of it.'

He turned when she answered him, and the compassion in her eyes tugged at his heart. How did she continue to see through him?

'But mostly I've kept it as it was when my parents were alive,' she pressed on, and took off her jersey, throwing it over one arm. 'My mom had great taste.'

'Yeah, she did.'

He was still thinking about her family when she said, 'I'm going to change. It shouldn't take too long, but feel free to make yourself comfortable.'

She walked through a doorway in the kitchen and he heard her footsteps on the floor and a door closing. He turned back to the shelf with the pictures and tried to keep his mind off the thought of her changing in the next room. But his thoughts kept shifting back to how she would be slipping off those heels that made her legs look as if they never ended. And she was probably taking off that dress that had done nothing to hide the curves that had been in his thoughts ever since he'd touched them.

He swallowed, and walked to the kitchen to pour himself a glass of water.

There was an empty glass in the sink, and he rinsed it and filled it with water from the tap. As he drank he looked up through the window that was just above the L-shaped kitchen counter. It overlooked a tidy little yard which was completely free of flowers, but had a large palm tree that shadowed a swing seat just beneath it. But the real view was of the mountain just above it.

'That's Lion's Head.'

He turned back to see Callie looking past him through the window. She had changed into a long floral skirt and a mint-green T-shirt, and had loosened her hair so that it fell in waves down her back. She looked so effortlessly beautiful that his heart stopped for a few minutes just looking at her. She walked towards him until she was next to him and then pointed to the right of the mountain he'd seen.

'Table Mountain is over there.'

But he couldn't keep his eyes off her, and her proximity overwhelmed his senses. When she looked back to him her eyes widened in that way they did whenever something she hadn't expected happened.

He put his hands on her waist, cautiously, asking permission without saying a word, and she took a step towards him so that there was barely any space between them. His arms slipped around her and his body heated at finally being able to feel hers again, and then he leaned down to her until his mouth was next to her ear.

'I'm going to kiss you now,' he whispered, and felt her shudder. He moved his head back so he could see her face, flushed and beautiful, and asked, 'Is that okay?'

'Yes.'

She had barely said the word before his lips were on hers. She had expected hunger, passion—everything that had burned with their first kiss. But there was none of that. Instead it felt as though he was trying to make up for that, to show her there was more to whatever was going on between them than just pure lust.

She thought vaguely that this might be the way their kiss on the rooftop would have felt if they'd let it continue for a while longer. And as the sweetness of their kiss swept through her she felt her heart open and be filled with it. He pulled her closer, and her heart beat at double its speed as she let her hands explore his body.

As soon as she did, the sweetness turned into need and she deepened their kiss, wanting more.

'Callie.'

Blake had ended the kiss, but he didn't let her go. She opened her eyes to see his own were closed, and he leaned his forehead against her.

'Do you want to give me a heart attack?'

She laughed breathlessly. 'I'm sorry. I didn't realise I had that in me.'

He lifted his head and smiled, and for the first time she noticed the crinkles around his eyes. She'd never really seen them before, she thought, and brushed a thumb across one of them.

'I think you have a lot in you that you don't re-alise,' he responded, and then took a deliberate step away from her.

As he did so she suddenly realised where she was, who she was with. Where had all this come from? Why was he was saying all the right things? About how she wasn't alone, how she shouldn't worry about the hotel, how they would deal with whatever was happening between them together. She had let her guard down enough to invite him in, and now he'd kissed her—in her own kitchen.

She turned her back to him and braced her hands on the sink as the uncertainty of the situation overwhelmed her.

'Hey,' Blake said, and moved to next to her. 'What's going on?'

'Nothing.' She turned to him and forced a smile to her face. 'Can I get you something to drink?'

'Callie, come on. I thought we agreed we were going to be open with one another.'

'Yeah, we did. So tell me where all this is coming from. How are you so calm and determined to be open with me when the last time you did this you pushed me away?'

The words had rushed from her mouth and she sighed, wishing she had some semblance of control over it. Especially when she saw the pain on his face.

'I'm sorry, Blake. I told you I was feeling a bit raw. And kissing doesn't help.' She resisted the urge to touch her lips.

He nodded. 'You're right. We should probably straighten things out before we do that again.'

Her heart accelerated even at the thought of it.

'Is that drink still up for offer?'

'Sure. Would you like some wine? I have a really good red.'

'Yeah, that's great.'

She poured the wine and joined him on the couch. It overlooked the garden when the curtains were open, and the amount of light it offered the house meant she kept them that way most of the time.

She handed him his glass and took a sip of her own wine as she snuggled into the corner of the couch. There was enough space between them that she felt safe from doing something she would likely regret if she were any closer.

'The last time I messed things up between us it was because of my ex-wife.'

He spoke suddenly, and Callie didn't know what to make of the way her stomach clenched at his mention of the woman. So she just nodded, and waited for him to continue.

'She was one of my employees at the Port Elizabeth Elegance Hotel. I met her a few years after my father retired, when I realised that the hotel in PE was losing staff at an incredibly high rate. I arranged a meeting with HR and they sent Julia.'

Callie watched as the tension on Blake's face tightened. She wanted to reach out to him, but she resisted. He needed to tell her about this without any help. But he had stopped talking.

She waited, then finally she asked, 'What was it that made you fall for her?'

He looked at her, and she saw a mixture of emotions in his eyes. Emotions that almost mirrored her own. She didn't really want to hear about what it was that had attracted Blake to this woman. But she needed to if they were going to make any progress together.

Then he exhaled sharply. 'I don't exactly know, to be honest with you. I guess it was because she had all the ingredients of the perfect woman. She was smart and beautiful, and I was attracted to her. But I didn't want to date her because— well...' he smiled wryly '...I was her boss.'

He continued now without any help, and she thought it was almost a compulsion for him to tell her.

'But professionalism didn't really mean as

much to me back then, so after about six months of resisting I asked her out. And it felt good. But what drew me in was Brent—her son.'

Blake didn't look at Callie but he paused, as though letting her process what he was telling her. She already had so many questions, but she refused to speak. Especially when she didn't think she would have the voice to do so.

After a few more moments he continued. 'She had always been honest with me about him. She'd told me that his father hadn't been in the picture from the beginning and that she'd been raising him by herself. And the way she told me that...'

He leaned forward now, bracing his elbows on his knees, and Callie realised he had long ago placed his wine, untouched, on the coffee table in front of them,

'That was, I think, what made me fall in love with her. She had this softness about her when she spoke about Brent that seemed so out of place in this woman who was all sass all the time.'

Callie didn't realise she was holding her breath until he looked at her, and the torment she saw in his eyes made her untangle her legs from under her and move closer to him. They sat there for a while in silence, and Callie thought about what he'd said. She remembered the way his eyes had dimmed when she'd spoken to him of his mother on the boat, what felt like a lifetime ago. It was quite simple for her to come to a conclusion then.

'She was a good mother. So different to what you'd had.' She hadn't realised she'd spoken out loud until he took a shaky breath.

'Yeah, I think that was it. And when I met Brent I fell in love with him, too. He reminded me a lot of myself.' He frowned, as though unsure of where that had come from. 'In hindsight, I suppose I fell for Brent more than I did for Julia, but they were intertwined. And then one day I found her crying in my office. She told me that she didn't think she was a good enough mother to Brent, that she wasn't giving him stability because he didn't have a father. And just like that she had me.'

He pushed off from the couch so fast that Callie felt her heart stop.

'I thought she was being honest with me. That she was being unselfish, thinking of her son first. Maybe she was. But the way she did it...' He shook his head.

She'd shown her son all the things Blake hadn't had growing up, Callie thought, and wished she could have been there for him then.

'I fell for it. I comforted her, told her she was an amazing mother, and started making plans to propose. I'd only known her for a year then, had been dating her for six months, and I *married* her.'

He looked at her, and she thought she saw embarrassment in his eyes.

'I married a woman I barely knew because she pulled at my heartstrings. My father insisted that we sign a prenuptial agreement, and we did—though she made some noise about that. The right noise, too. About how we didn't need a prenup when we were going to last. We were a family, and we were going to make it work. And for a year we did.'

He joined her on the couch again, and Callie took his hand, wanting to provide as much comfort as she could.

'Callie, I didn't think I would *ever* be as happy as I was being a husband and a father. We were a family. *I* had a family.' He rubbed a hand across his face. 'But I was in a bubble, and I only noticed the way Julia had changed when it began to affect Brent. She had become snarky and mean. Only to me, luckily, but she was doing it in front of Brent, and I could tell that he hated it. When I challenged her on it she told me it was none of my business because Brent wasn't even my son.

He looked at her, and then lowered his eyes.

'I tried to save the relationship—I really did. I even went so far as to look into adopting Brent. I hired an investigator to find Brent's father so that I could ask him to relinquish his parental rights to me. I was going to surprise Julia with it. But then one night she told me it wasn't working, and that what was happening between us was hurting Brent. That was the last thing I wanted, so I agreed to a divorce. I had just wanted to give Brent a home, a family.'

'I'm so sorry, Blake.' Callie spoke because she had to. She couldn't take the pain in his voice any longer.

He looked at her now, smiled sadly. 'Thanks, but I was in that relationship for the wrong reasons. For my own reasons. Julia had her reasons, too, so we were both wrong—though I do think she thought she was doing the right thing for

Brent. She wanted to make sure that he never lacked for money.'

'Wait—what?'

Blake shot her a confused look. And then he nodded. 'Oh, yeah, I didn't mention that. When we spoke about the divorce she told me she had only married me so that she could live the life she knew she and her son deserved. And then she realised that she was hurting him instead, and she didn't want that.' He shook his head. 'That was pretty much the end of it.'

'Did she get anything in the divorce?' Callie didn't want to ask, but it was one of the pieces of the puzzle she needed to understand him better.

'No, the prenup prevented that. And Brent didn't either, since the contract stated he needed to be legally mine before I was required to pay anything.'

'Do you still see him?'

'No, I don't. Julia resigned shortly after we divorced and moved to back to Namibia, where she's from.'

'Blake...' Callie shifted over and put an arm around him. 'I'm sorry.'

He lifted his own arm, put it around her, and sat

back so that she could lay her head on his chest. They sat like that for a while, and Callie wished she had words to say that would take the pain away. Suddenly everything made sense to her. His resistance to dating an employee. His pushing her away when she got too close. He was broken inside, and he didn't want anyone to know.

'I've created a trust fund for him.' Blake spoke softly. 'When he's twenty-five—old enough to decide what to do with his own money—he'll get something from me. It may not mean much to him—'

'But you needed to do it.' She leaned back and watched him nod, before putting her head on his chest again. 'You're a good man, Blake Owen.'

CHAPTER THIRTEEN

CALLIE LOOKED AT HERSELF in the mirror and tried to be critical. She was wearing a blue floral dress with a white jersey and matching heels, and her hair was tied into a loose bun. She had to lead a meeting about the gala event that day, and she wanted to look her best. She placed a hand on her nervous stomach and forced herself to admit that she wanted to look her best for Blake, too.

He hadn't stayed for very long after they'd spoken last night. Callie knew that telling her about his past had made him feel uncomfortable, so she hadn't pushed him. Instead she'd brushed a kiss on his cheek and waved him away, all the while worrying about what it meant for *them*. She could no longer deny that there was something between them, but even the thought of it terrified her. Especially as they hadn't defined it yet, and she didn't even know how long Blake would be staying in Cape Town.

Or if he would be staying at all.

She shook her head and told herself that there was no point in worrying about it now, when everything was still so new and fresh. She would just have to wait and see how it played out. She sighed, and wished that was enough for her.

She grabbed her handbag when she heard a car hoot outside and locked up quickly, not wanting Connor to wait. Her car would probably be ready after the weekend, her mechanic had told her, and he had also cautioned her that it didn't have much life left in it. This she knew—though part of her wanted to keep it, even if she left it in the garage, just because it reminded her of the days when she had been part of a family.

'Hey, Cals. How are you?' Connor asked as she climbed into the car and kissed him on the cheek.

'Fine—no thanks to you. What were you thinking, throwing me to the wolves yesterday?' Callie wasn't sure why she'd said that, but somehow she felt it was what he would expect her to say if she hadn't shared anything personal with their boss.

'Sorry about that.'

He grimaced and she thought her gut instinct had been right.

'Urgent matter at home.'

She looked at him in alarm. 'Is everything all right?'

'Not really.' Connor focused hard on the road ahead of him and didn't even look her way.

'Connor,' she said, in the stern voice she only used with him, 'what's going on?'

After a few more moments of silence he said tersely, 'Elizabeth is pregnant.'

Her jaw dropped before she consciously realised. 'Oh, Connor…'

'She only found out a few days ago. Told me yesterday.' He shrugged, though the movement was heavy with tension. 'I guess I'm going to be a dad.'

Callie wished she had the right words for him, but she didn't. Connor had been dating Elizabeth for less than six months. And, while she was a perfectly lovely girl, she knew Connor didn't want to start a family this way. Family was a responsibility that deserved attention, and she and Connor had lived by that because that was the way *they* had been raised.

Her heart cracked for him, but she knew that

all she could do was offer her support. 'How do you feel about this?'

'I'm not sure. I think I'm still a little numb from the shock. It wasn't planned.'

She laughed a little. 'Yeah, I got *that* part.'

He gave her a wry smile, and then sobered. 'But...I *want* it, Cals. I want to keep the baby. And so does she. You know how much family means to me. And after Mom and Dad died I thought I'd lost that. Do you know what I mean?'

'Yes, I do.'

'Now I get to have my own...and I don't think that's a *bad* thing.'

'Of course it isn't!' She felt excitement bubble inside her at the prospect of seeing her brother as a father. And ignored the voice in her head that threatened to temper it. 'I think you're going to be an amazing father. I mean, an amazing brother, not so much—but definitely an amazing father!'

He laughed, and she could tell some of the tension had gone from him. Feeling an urge to make even more of it go away, she placed a hand over his and said, 'I think Mom and Dad would be so proud of you. There's no doubt in my mind that you're going to give your child what they gave us—a good, solid, wonderful family.'

He smiled at her, and they drove the rest of the way to the hotel in silence.

She'd meant every word she had said to him. She could picture Connor running around with a little boy or girl in the backyard, could see herself spending holidays with him and his family. So why did she feel so strange? Perhaps it was because she wished her parents could have been there to see their grandchildren? Yes, she knew there was some truth in that. But something niggled inside her, and she knew that wasn't quite all of it.

No, she thought suddenly, it was because now she wondered where *she* would fit into Connor's new life.

Something inside her broke, though she couldn't explain why. But before she could examine it they'd arrived at the hotel.

'Thank you.'

'Of course. Cals?' Connor looked over at her. 'Are you okay?'

She forced her doubts and her fears away, and smiled over at him. 'Yeah.' She got out of the car and hugged him when he joined her. 'It's going to be okay, Connor. I promise.'

She repeated the words to herself as she walked to her office, and then tried to force the situation out of her mind altogether so that she could focus on preparing for the meeting in less than an hour.

But her mind kept wandering, until finally she sighed and went to get herself a cup of coffee. Before she got to the kitchen she saw a flurry of activity around it, like bees weaving in and out of a beehive, and did a neat three-sixty turn and instead headed for the conference room.

Her heart beat a little faster as she knocked at the door, and it accelerated one hundredfold when she heard the muffled, 'Come in.'

'Hey,' she said as she walked in.

'Hi.' Blake smiled at her, and stood up at the end of the table. 'What are you doing here? I thought you were going to prepare for the meeting in your own office.'

'I was, but then I couldn't really focus and I needed coffee. And, since nowadays coffee in the kitchen comes with the dozens of questions my colleagues seem to have every time they see me, I thought I might persuade you to share.'

'No persuasion needed.' He grinned and walked to the counter to grab a mug. 'Can I pour you some?'

She nodded, and wordlessly took in how attractive he looked. She would never tire of it, she thought. Admiring him in a suit was definitely on the list of things that she most enjoyed doing.

'Black, one sugar, right?'

She shook herself, and blushed when she saw the amused look on his face. 'Yes, please.'

She walked to one of the conference room chairs and sat heavily, needing a moment to process everything. She was all over the place, she thought, and forced herself to be *present*. To be in the moment. She had so many important things to do. Her job depended on the tours she still had to do this week, and so did her brother's. And while she *was* struggling with processing her brother's announcement, she still wanted to support him. One of the biggest ways she could do that was to fight for the hotel he loved…and the job that he needed if he was going to be a father.

Then there was Blake, and all her feelings for him that were knotted in a ball at the base of her stomach. She took a deep breath in, and exhaled slowly.

'Hey, is everything okay?'

Blake handed her the coffee and sat on the chair next to hers.

'Thanks,' she said, and then answered him. 'Everything is fine. Just the usual concerns.' She smiled, but she could feel that it was off.

'About the event?'

She nodded, because she didn't know what else to do.

'Look, I know this isn't your thing. I remember the night we met Connor mentioned it was out of your comfort zone,' he elaborated when she looked up in surprise. 'Which makes me respect your suggestion for doing it all the more. But you don't have to worry. After the meeting today we'll know exactly where we stand with the planning, and we can take it from there.'

She stared blankly at the cup of coffee in her hands, and blew at the steam in an attempt to cool it down. She had heard him, but her thoughts had almost immediately drifted away to Connor's situation. What would it mean for *their* relationship? She knew his child would come first, of course, but would that mean that she would lose him, too?

'Callie?'

'Mmm?' She looked up at Blake and realised he was waiting for a response when she saw the questioning look on his face.

'Yes, I know it's going to be fine.' She laid a hand on his cheek, finding the warmth there comforting, and then stood. 'I need to prepare. Thanks for the coffee.'

'Are you sure you're okay?'

'I'm fine.' She brushed a kiss on his lips. 'I'll see you at the meeting.'

She walked out the door, her mind already wandering back to Connor.

Blake leaned against his car and resisted the urge to pace.

Callie had been so unlike herself today that he had wanted to corner her as soon as he could to demand that she give him something other than her generic 'I'm fine.' He hated to think that it was about him, but after what he had shared with her the previous evening, the thought kept strolling through his head, making him restless.

He knew he hadn't stayed very long after he'd told her about Julia, but he'd thought it was best for them to spend some time apart to process what had just happened. Because something had shifted between them, and he'd wanted to give her space—and, yes, give himself space too—to come to terms with it.

He hadn't worried that he'd done the wrong thing until he'd seen her in the conference room. She'd been pale, and her usual vibrant demeanour had seemed almost brittle. She had looked... *fragile.*

Again he despised the thought that it might have been because of him. But the more he'd seen of her that day, the more he'd thought that it might be. She had still been professional—she had handled the meeting with a grace and leadership that had had him thinking about her future at Elegance—but underneath it he'd been able to see that something was wrong.

So he had gone rogue and told Connor that Callie would be working late that night, that he shouldn't worry about getting her home because Blake would drop her. Connor had dubiously accepted, but had thankfully been distracted enough not to verify it with Callie. He knew the man had been under a lot of strain lately, and there were rings under his eyes that looked like thunderclouds. But it would be over soon enough, and none of his employees would have to worry about their future any more.

He looked at his watch and wondered if Callie had got his message that *he* would be taking her home. He was just about to call when he heard the click of heels coming towards him. He looked up and was blown away by her beauty all over again. He had been right that first night they'd met, he thought, about her walking as though on a red carpet. She was so graceful, so elegant, that it made him square his shoulders and take his hands out his pockets.

She looked up at him and smiled—an utterly exhausted smile, but a smile nevertheless—and tightened her grip on the handbag under her arm.

'Are you making up for lost time with these lifts?' she asked easily, and something in Blake's heart released.

'Maybe. Or maybe I just like seeing if I can trick your brother into forgetting how protective he is of you.'

Her smile dimmed, and then she said, 'We should probably get going.'

Blake frowned, wondering what he had said wrong, but he opened the car door and waited as she got in. Then he decided to drive to his house instead.

She didn't say a word to him—not even when he drove in completely the opposite direction to her house. She only looked up when the gates to his house opened.

'Where are we?'

'My place. I figured I could make you some dinner.'

She looked at him in surprise. 'You *cook*?'

'Yes, I do. And I'll try not to be offended by the incredulity in your eyes.' He smiled at her. 'Do you have anything against steak?'

CHAPTER FOURTEEN

CALLIE TRIED TO KEEP a neutral expression on her face as she looked up at the place where Blake lived.

The house was a combination of brick and glass, with brown frames outlining the doors and windows. A deck on the upper level of the house overlooked a vast estate, including a small pond that Callie could see from where she was standing outside his car. She walked forward, caught a glimpse of the city lights, and imagined that standing on his deck would be quite an experience.

When Blake had unlocked the large oak door he stepped aside for her to walk past and her neutral expression gave way to a jaw-drop.

Brick walls, wooden furniture and sparks of green were scattered across the living room in a design that screamed warmth. A fireplace was the focal point of the room—and rightly so, she thought as she took in its impressive design, and then walked through the room to a passage that opened onto the kitchen and dining room.

The kitchen space was huge, and had the same homely yet modern design as the living room. Granite counters were highlighted by pops of colour and a window looked out onto a garden that made her salivate. The dining room was more elegant—wooden floors and a black dining room set that was decked out with cutlery and crockery that looked incredibly expensive.

'This is not what I expected from you.'

'Did you think I lived in a cold black and white room?' He smirked as he said it, but his eyes grew serious when she nodded.

'Something like that. This is a lot more...*inviting* than I expected.'

He looked around, as though seeing it for the first time. 'It is, isn't it? Though it's wasted on me. I've barely spent any time here, and the decor was pretty much left to the interior designer I hired.'

'Perhaps they decorated according to what they thought the house needed instead of thinking about its owner.'

He narrowed his eyes. 'I'm not sure if you just complimented me or insulted me.'

She laughed, and felt a bit of the tension of the day leave her. 'I was only agreeing with you that this house needs to be somewhere people are invited to.' She ran a hand over the kitchen counter. 'It deserves a family.'

The words felt fatalistic as she said them, and although she knew why it felt that way for her, she wasn't sure what the expression on Blake's face meant.

Then it cleared and he smiled. 'Well, you haven't seen the second floor, where I spend most of my time. It's a lot colder than this.'

He winked and she laughed.

'Now, shall we have some supper?'

She nodded, and settled back on a bar stool at the kitchen counter. Though she wanted to offer her help, there was something about watching him go through the motions of making a meal that helped soothe the turmoil inside her. She also wanted to speak, to tell him of all that was going through her head, but she couldn't bring herself to interrupt what seemed surprisingly easy for him. So she just sat and watched him—watched as he spiced the meat, seared it in a pan, and popped it into the oven.

He took out two wine glasses, poured a liberal amount of wine into each, and handed a glass to her.

'Now, will you tell me what's happening in that head of yours?'

'What do you mean?' she asked, but she didn't look him in the eye.

'Callie, come on. You and I both know you've been distracted today. We promised each other we would be open.'

She looked up at him when he paused, and felt alarm go through her as he clenched his teeth.

'If this is because of Julia, then—'

'What?' she exclaimed, and then she placed her wine down and walked around the counter until she was in front of him. She brushed the piece of hair he should really have cut out of his face and kept her hand on his cheek for a moment. 'No, Blake. This isn't about Julia—or you.'

He took her hands and squeezed. 'Then what's wrong?'

She bit her lip and then she said, very softly, 'Connor is going to be a father.'

* * *

Blake felt his eyebrows lift, and then carefully rearranged his features. 'And that's a *bad* thing?'

'No, I don't think so.'

She walked back around the counter, and Blake thought it might be symbolic, somehow, her placing an obstacle between them.

'I mean, it isn't the *best* thing that could happen to him right now, what with our jobs being on the line and him only knowing his girlfriend for six months...'

This time Blake didn't try to hide his surprise, and Callie grinned at him.

'That's not like the man you thought you knew so well, is it?'

'No, it isn't.' He looked up at her, and saw something in her eyes that prompted him to ask, 'Or is it?'

'I'm beginning to think it is.'

She lifted her wine glass slowly, not meeting his eye. And when she did, he saw a flash of pain that quickly settled into something he couldn't quite identify.

'I mean, not the getting-a-girl-pregnant thing. But the baby...' She trailed off. 'I think it helped

Connor cope with my parents' deaths when he had to help *me.*'

'What do you mean?'

She looked at him, then sighed. 'Should we be making a salad, or something else to go with the steak?'

He didn't respond, recognising her ploy, but walked to the fridge and started removing vegetables. He was glad he had made a visit to the shop the day before—he'd wanted steak and his conscience had guilted him into buying the ingredients for a salad. He'd have to do it more often if Callie visited regularly.

And then he stopped, remembering her earlier words about his house needing family, and something nudged at him. But he forced it away and handed her cherry tomatoes and an avocado to cut. Before he knew it—and, he thought, before she was ready—they were done.

'Nothing left to distract you now,' he said, and laid a hand on her cheek. 'Tell me.'

She sighed again, walked back around the counter and sat down. Then she spoke without looking at him. 'I just mean that family has always *meant* something to Connor. To both of us, really, but to him most of all. And when our parents died they left a void that we both felt.' She paused. 'I thought that we'd filled it for one another. But I think this baby is going to do it for him.'

Blake watched her as she spoke. Her shoulders were tight, and he realised that she was embarrassed by what she was saying. Suddenly it clicked.

'And you're going to be left alone?'

She didn't look up at him, but he thought he saw a tear roll down her cheek.

'Yeah, that's it. Except that admitting it makes me sound selfish.'

Before she had finished speaking Blake pulled her into his arms. He wanted to comfort her—needed to, perhaps—because he was feeling less and less comfortable with what she was saying and he wasn't sure why. So he focused on her, and said what he thought she needed to hear.

'Callie, I know that Connor helped you get through your parents' deaths. And you have every right to be grateful to him for that. But he isn't the reason you got through it.' He leaned back so he could look into her eyes. '*You* are.'

She blinked, and two more tears escaped from her eyes. 'Connor *did* help me get through my parents' deaths.' She said it slowly, deliberately, as though trying to convince him of the fact.

'I know he did. But just because he helped you, it doesn't mean he's the *reason* you made it through.'

He repeated it, stopping only to check how his words were affecting her.

'Callie, when you told me about how you dealt with everything you said that *you* were the one who became interested in your job. *You* chose to start interacting with the guests. *You* were the one who took the initiative to start tours. Connor could never have forced you to do it, even if he'd waited outside your house every single day for a year.'

He stopped, trying to gauge whether she was taking it in.

'I know Connor is important to you, and that the two of you have been through a lot together, but that doesn't mean you can't do it alone. Besides, you won't be alone.'

She looked up at him now, and the hope in her eyes knocked him in the gut.

'I mean, I don't think Connor won't be there for you any more just because he's having a baby.' He said the words quickly, for reasons he didn't want to examine. Not when they were so entwined with feelings he couldn't explain. The hope in her eyes was quickly dimmed, and although he knew he had spoken in response to that hope its extinguishment disappointed him.

'Yeah, maybe you're right,' she said, and was quiet as she waited for him to dish up.

And even though the meal was one of his favourites to make on the rare occasions he was at home, he didn't taste it. His thoughts were too busy with why he had tried to back out of the support he wanted to offer her.

'I think I forgot that Connor's baby will be my family, too.'

Callie spoke softly, and dragged him from his thoughts. Her expression was pensive, but when she met his eyes there was a sparkle there that had been missing the entire day.

'I've been thinking selfishly all day.'

'Your reaction was completely normal. You weren't being selfish.'

'Maybe normal, but definitely selfish.'

She smiled at him, and his lips curved in response. 'Maybe just a little.'

She laughed lightly, cut another piece from her steak, and then looked at him. 'You're the first person who's ever made me feel like it's okay to be alone. Or that I might have helped *myself* get out of my depression. Thank you.'

Her words were so sincere that they ripped at his heart, and immediately he felt like a fraud. He didn't deserve her gratitude when he couldn't even tell her that he would be there for her. When her simple comments about family had frozen him up.

'You're welcome.'

They ate the rest of their meal in silence, each lost in thought, and when they were done she ran the water for washing the dishes. He sat back, watching her as she pulled plates into the soapy water, rinsed them, and then placed them on the dish rack. Slowly, almost without realising it, he began to picture her there after a long day at work.

He could almost see the rain outside the window above where she was washing up, could hear the fire roaring in the living room. He even saw himself walking to her and offering a hand, drawing her close to him as he touched her stomach, where she was carrying their child…

'You know, I think before today I hadn't thought about family outside of my parents and brother. But it's nice to think that we could expand.'

He was ripped out of his fantasy, felt his heart racing faster than he'd thought possible. 'Yeah?'

'Yeah.' She turned to him and her expression softened. 'Wasn't your time with Brent good?'

His heart still pounded as he answered her. 'Yes, it was.'

'I thought so.' She nodded, and started washing again. 'Connor's going to be an amazing father. And being an aunt won't be so bad.'

It was almost as though she was thinking out loud.

'I'll get to practise for when I have my own kids one day. *Ha!* I hadn't even thought about having my own family until now.'

'Do you *want* to have a family?' he asked, before he could stop himself. He didn't think he would have been able to stop himself even if he'd had the chance. Not when he still saw that picture of her pregnant in their house—no, *his* house—vividly in his mind.

She turned around and wiped her hands with a dry cloth. 'Yeah—yeah, I think I do.' She tilted her head and said, 'It's our legacy, I guess.' She smiled at him. 'Building on the foundation of family that our parents gave us.'

The words hit him right in the stomach, and finally he realised what it was that was bothering him. *Family*. The word that described his biggest disappointments. And now, he thought in panic, his biggest fear.

'Callie, do you mind if I take you home?' he asked, and ignored the voice in his head that called him a coward. 'It's getting late and I still have a couple of things to do before our next proposal tomorrow.'

'Um…okay—sure,' she said, and his heart clenched when he saw her bewildered expression.

He helped her with the dishes in silence as he tried to work through the thoughts in his head. He wanted it. Family. With Callie. Never before had he felt a need more intense. Never before had he seen something this clearly. But he'd lost things before. Things that hadn't meant nearly as much to him. And those things had nearly broken him.

Like Brent, he thought as they made their way to the car. He'd loved that boy more than he'd thought he could, and his heart was still raw from not being near him. And like his parents, who had both, in their own way, left him. He fought the memories of those heartbreaks every day, still carried the scars of them with him.

More so than he had realised, he thought, remembering his conversation with Callie on the boat when she had pointed it out to him.

If somehow this didn't work out between them—if, for some reason, Callie left him—he knew he wouldn't be able to go on as though nothing had happened. No, he would be a broken man. And she would carry the pieces of him with her, so that he would never be able to put himself together again.

And even if she didn't leave he would risk disappointing her. He knew nothing about family. Nothing about the foundation she spoke of—her *legacy*. He didn't have much to contribute to that. His mother had left him and his father was more business partner than parent.

It didn't matter that he wanted to be a part of her life, he thought sadly, and it didn't matter that he wanted to have a family with her. What mattered was that he would fail her—just as he had Brent. And he knew that it would kill him if he failed her. And more importantly, he realised, it would devastate him to hurt her like that.

'Hey, what's going on?' she said softly, taking one of his hands.

Blake turned to her and realised that he had pulled up in front of her driveway. He wondered when that had happened.

'Nothing,' he answered, feeling his heart hurting from the lie, but knowing it was for the best.

The only way to avoid disappointing, failing or hurting her—*and* himself—was to put some distance between them. And, though it killed him, that meant not talking to her about the way he felt. Not when he still needed to figure out what to do about it.

'Really?' she scoffed. 'So we've been sitting here for ten minutes for you to think about *nothing*?'

He resisted the urge to tell her what was wrong, and forced himself to think about the look on

Brent's face the last time Blake had seen him. The memory of the mixture of emotions in the little boy's eyes—especially the heartbreak—helped him steel his heart.

He *never* wanted to see that expression on Callie's face.

'It's just been a long day, that's all.'

She looked at him for a while, and then moved her hands to her lap. 'So, is this "being open" you reminded me of earlier something that only *I* have to follow?'

Though his heart tightened at the emotion in her voice, he ignored it. He was doing the only thing that would protect both of them. 'Look, there really isn't anything going on. I've just had a long day, and I still need to get things done. I was thinking about that.' He tried to smile, but knew he was failing miserably at it.

'Fine. If that's what you're going with.'

She picked up her bag and got out of the car, but the tiny moment of relief Blake felt was shattered when she slammed the door shut.

'Callie.'

He got out quickly, not knowing what he could

say—not when he wanted space to think about everything—yet he needed her to be okay with him.

'Please.'

She stopped on the first step of the path up to her house and then turned to him. He knew the hurt in her eyes was a picture that would stay with him through the night.

'Look, if you need time to work through whatever's going on, that's fine. But don't lie to me about it.'

He walked towards her, but stuffed the hands that itched to take hers into his pockets.

'Okay.' He paused, then exhaled slowly. 'I need time.'

She nodded. 'Okay.' She kissed his cheek and walked to her house, shutting the door after a slight wave.

And for a long time afterwards Blake stood outside her house, thinking about the choice he needed to make and why he needed to make it.

CHAPTER FIFTEEN

IT WAS FINALLY FRIDAY, the day was gorgeous, and the final arrangements for the gala event were going well.

It was being held on the Elegance's rooftop—an idea Callie had had after she and Blake had gone for the tasting. It had taken some planning—and a lot of convincing—to change the venue so soon before the event, but as she looked around she was glad she'd managed it.

Pillars stood at each corner of the rooftop, with mini-lanterns draped between them. A stage had been set up at one end, adorned with light. The band they'd hired were setting up there, and any speeches during the evening would be made from it. Tables had been set around the centre of the roof, with white flower centrepieces and napkins on black tablecloths, leaving space for a dance floor. The food would be plated, there was a bar up and ready, and the bustle of the staff doing the final touches should have given Callie a sense of accomplishment.

Except that as she stood there, looking at everything, she wasn't feeling anything except dread.

All she'd been able to think about for the last few days was the way Blake had decided to take her home after the dinner they'd had at his house. The way he'd lied to her about what was bothering him. And although she told herself to be patient, although she reassured herself that he would tell her when he was ready, every time she saw him the feeling of dread deepened.

Because somehow she knew he was slipping away from her.

She'd tried to brush it off at first as paranoia. He wasn't acting differently around her—at least not on the surface. But her heart knew that there were no more lingering looks, no more affectionate touches. Those had been replaced with smiles that had no depth and words that didn't say what he meant. She'd hidden the hurt, hidden the concern, and waited in vain for him to tell her what was wrong.

And the wait was breaking her.

'It's amazing.'

She turned to see Blake surveying the area. He offered her a smile, and again she was struck by how different it was.

'Yeah, I can't believe we actually pulled it off.' She looked around again, and then returned his smile tentatively. 'I think it's going to be a success.'

He nodded, and she saw something flash across his eyes.

And then he said, 'Shouldn't you be busy with your hair? We only have four more hours until the event. You're cutting it close.'

She tilted her head, trying to figure out his mood. 'No, I have my things downstairs. I'll get ready once I'm sure everything is done up here.'

He stuffed his hands into his pockets. 'I was joking, Callie.'

'Were you?' She shrugged, ignoring the pain in her heart. 'I can't seem to tell with you lately.'

'Look,' he said, and then took a deep breath.

He stood in silence for a moment—his hands still in his pockets, his face tense—and Callie felt her nails cutting into her hands as she clenched her fists, waiting for him.

'Did you say you have your things downstairs?'

'What?'

'You don't have an afternoon of pampering planned after this week?'

'No, Blake, I don't.' She brushed off the irritability that threatened. 'I didn't have time to make the appointments this week nor do I want to spend a ridiculous amount of money on a new dress—'

'You don't have a dress to wear tonight?' he interrupted her.

'Of course I do,' she said defensively. 'It's just not new. It's one of my mom's. But what does that have to do with anything?'

Callie was ashamed of the desperation that coated her tone.

He looked at her for a few moments, and then pulled out his phone, his fingers speeding over the screen. A 'ping' sounded almost immediately, and he nodded and put it back into his pocket. Then he looked at her, and something in his eyes softened her heart.

'Would you come with me?'

His voice was hesitant, as though he wasn't quite sure of what she was going to say. That, combined with the look in his eyes, made her insides crumble, and she took the hand he offered. Even though everything inside her wanted to say no, wanted to ask him why he was allowing this uncertainty to eat at them, she let him lead her down the stairs.

And felt hopeless when the thought that she would follow him anywhere flitted through her mind.

They didn't speak when they reached the parking garage, and she waited for him as he moved to open the car door for her. But his hand stilled on the handle and he stepped back.

'What's wrong?' she asked—and then she saw the look in his eyes and felt herself tremble.

She was standing just behind the front door of the car, and when he took a step towards her instinct had her moving back against it. Her heart thudded as his hands slid around her waist and he pulled her closer, until she was moulded to his body. She looked up at him, breathless, and her knees nearly gave way at the need, the desperation in his eyes.

She closed her own eyes when he moved his head—closed them against the onslaught of emotions that flooded through her at the look on his face—and thought that their kiss would be filled with hunger, with the passion that need brought.

But instead it was so tender that she nearly wept. She slid her hands through his hair and shivers went down her spine when he deepened their kiss, taking more. She felt herself being swept away with it, but her heart cracked, just a little, as she thought that he must be trying to memorise the way she tasted, the way she felt.

Her heart demanded the same, and she slowly opened the buttons of his shirt and slid her hands up and down his chest, over his abs and back up again. She shook when the muscles beneath her hands trembled.

And then he moved back, breathing heavily, with his forehead against hers. She realised that she was breathing heavily too, and she stepped away from him, laying a hand on her racing heart. Finally, time and place caught up with her and she looked around, half expecting to see a colleague looking at them with shock. But the parking garage was empty, and for some strange reason she felt disappointment.

'I'm sorry,' he said, and she saw that he had buttoned his shirt up.

'Why are you apologising?' she asked, and braced herself for his answer.

But he simply said that someone might have seen them, and she nodded, not trusting herself to speak when she realised *why* she felt disappointed that no one had.

Because now there was no proof that everything that had happened between her and Blake hadn't only been in her head.

He opened the car door for her, and when he'd got in he pulled out of the parking garage and started driving towards the business centre of Cape Town.

'Where are you taking me?' she asked, when she thought she had her thoughts—and her body—back under control.

'To a friend. You'll see when we get there,' he said quietly, and again Callie wondered what was going on with him. With them.

She had never felt this unsure in her life. Even when her parents had died she had had certainty. She'd known they were gone, and the only thing she'd been unsure of then had been herself. Now she was wondering if she'd made up their relationship—could she even call it that?—in her head. The feelings, the sharing… Had that just been wishful thinking? Was she just a fling to him? Someone to pass the time with?

No, she thought. That couldn't be it. Not when they'd shared things that she knew had been new for both of them. Besides, he'd never tried anything besides kissing with her. And, yes, the kissing had been hot and delicious, but he'd had the opportunity to press for more. Like the evening they'd been at his house… But instead he'd just dropped her off at home. That didn't seem like a man who wanted a fling.

But why hadn't he defined what they were? an inner voice asked her. He'd never told her that she was his girlfriend. A mistake, she realised, and suddenly she was immensely tired of the back and forth of her thoughts. She was going to ask him, once and for all. She would demand to know what they were to one another, and why he had pushed her away that night. She would demand the truth from him.

Satisfied with her resolution, she opened her mouth to speak—but the words stuck when he pulled up in front of two large bronze gates.

Blake pressed the buzzer and told the crackly voice who he was, and the gates opened.

Callie held her breath as they drove up the path and she saw the large white house in front of them. Blake pulled into one of the designated parking bays and they walked to the front door, barely having enough time to press the button before the door opened and a woman stepped out and pulled Blake into her arms.

Callie might have felt threatened if the woman had done it in a remotely flirtatious way. But her hug was almost maternal, and Callie felt interest prickle when the woman drew back and said, 'Let me take a look at you.' She scanned Blake from his head to his toes and back up again, and then she smiled, and Callie thought it made her look years younger. 'Blake, you're an adult. I can't believe it.'

He laughed. 'Yes, Caroline, I have been now for quite some time.'

'Which I would have known, had you visited me at any point during that time.' She gave him a stern look, and then waved a hand. 'But that's water under the bridge now that you're here.'

She turned and Callie felt her back stiffen as she was sized up.

'And who are *you*, darling?'

'This is Callie. She's...a friend of mine.' He paused, as though thinking about what he had called her, and then continued. 'She needs a new dress for an event at the hotel tonight.'

'Oh, why didn't you just say so? Come on, let's go in.'

She walked past the two of them down the passage, and entered a room right at the end. Callie and Blake followed, and she whispered, 'Who *is* this woman?'

'She's an old family friend. My mother's, actually, though she didn't want us to hold that against her when my mother left. Her name is Caroline Bellinger.'

Callie stopped in her tracks. 'You *know* Caroline Bellinger?'

'Yes. Why?'

'Why?' She looked at him incredulously. 'Caroline Bellinger is Cape Town's top designer. She's designed dresses for local celebrities for almost all of our glamourous events. She isn't just someone's "family friend".'

'Do you plan on joining me, or are you going to stand in the passage whispering about me all day?' Caroline called from the room.

Blake grinned. A genuine one this time, she noted.

'She's astute, isn't she? Come on, let's find you a dress for tonight.'

From that moment Callie felt as though she had been selected for a makeover show. Caroline examined her even more critically than she had when they'd met, and Callie had to resist the cringe that came over her when Caroline announced that she had a body 'like a movie star'. She could tell Blake was enjoying the show, but Caroline shooed him out before she pulled out any dresses.

'You can follow Darren, Blake. He'll take you to the restaurant where we make all the men wait while we do this.'

The man who appeared when his name was called nodded at Blake, and Blake gave Callie a reassuring nod before leaving. She held her breath when she realised that Caroline was now looking at her, and she felt the weight of the woman's stare.

'So, you and Blake are...*friends*?'

Caroline didn't believe it for a second, Callie thought, but answered, 'Yes, I think so.'

'I didn't need an answer, dear. I just wanted to see your face after my question.'

Caroline didn't elaborate on what she'd seen there, and walked past Callie to a rack of dresses on the other side of the room.

'I met another friend of Blake's a while ago. Except it was at their wedding.'

Callie quickly realised what Caroline was implying, and it had her shaking her head. 'No, no. This isn't anything like him and Julia.'

Caroline raised her eyebrows. 'No, it can't be if he's told you about her.'

She returned to Callie with four dresses, each of which looked as though they were fit for royalty.

'He didn't bring her here, you know.'

'Excuse me?'

Caroline handed her a midnight-blue dress that Callie worried might not cover nearly as much of her body as she would have liked before answering.

'I always thought I would be the one to make

Blake's bride's wedding dress. Though he didn't even ask me.' She looked at Callie again, and this time the gaze felt distinctly more piercing. 'And yet here you are. For a dress for an event at the hotel.' She paused again, and then simply said, 'You can get changed over there.'

She pointed to a dressing screen and Callie followed, not sure what else she was supposed to do. Or whether she was supposed to speak at all. The woman had given her so many innuendoes that Callie wasn't sure she was able to process them all.

She dressed as quickly as she could, and almost sighed when she felt the silk on her skin. It was luxurious, she thought, grateful for the distraction of something as simple as a dress. Except that this dress was anything *but* simple. She thought she could easily become used to such luxury...until she walked out and Caroline shook her head.

'Oh, *no*, that's dreadful.'

Callie felt her face blanch, but Caroline waved a hand.

'No, darling, it's not you—it's the combination of you and that dress. Try this one instead. I think it'll do wonders for that rich skin tone of yours. And it won't hide your curves either.'

She winked, and Callie took the dress wordlessly.

She knew that artists could be eccentric—but, honestly, she hadn't ever experienced it first-hand before. It was strange that this woman was a part of Blake's life. Her conservative boss—she'd settled on using that term, since she wasn't sure *what* to call him personally—didn't strike her as someone who would be familiar with a person so—well, *unique.* Especially when Caroline seemed to see things Callie didn't think most people would want her to see—especially not someone as private as Blake.

She looked down at the dress, noting how much tighter it was than the previous one, and resisted pulling at the neckline that lay just a touch too low for her liking. When she walked out in the emerald dress Caroline clasped her hands together in what Callie could only imagine was delight.

'This is *it.* This is the *one.*'

Callie doubted the dress required that much enthusiasm, and was still thinking about it when

Caroline asked her what size shoe she wore. She responded automatically, even though she wanted to tell the woman that she had some shoes she could wear with the dress. But then Caroline brought out the most gorgeous silver pair Callie had ever seen and she kept her mouth shut.

'Gorgeous—though there's something missing…' She looked at Callie for a few more moments, and then went to fetch something from a glass cabinet.

Callie didn't realise what it was until Caroline presented her with a diamond necklace.

'Oh, Caroline, I couldn't—'

'You can, and you will.' She fastened the necklace around Callie's neck herself, and then led her to the mirror.

Callie was almost afraid to look, but she caught her reflection before she had a chance to close her eyes and nearly gasped. She looked… *Wow*, she thought. Maybe the dress *had* required that much enthusiasm. She almost didn't recognise herself.

Caroline had been right about the colour, and the gown fitted her perfectly. The necklace sparkled up at her, matching the shoes that she could see beneath the slit that ran up her left leg. She had never seen herself like this before. Not even on the night of Blake's welcome event had she looked this elegant.

She remained silent when Caroline stood behind her and twisted her hair into some kind of chignon.

'You should wear your hair like this. And just a touch of make-up. We don't want to hide any of your natural beauty.'

Callie nodded wordlessly, not trusting herself to speak. What could she possibly say to this woman who had made her look like a princess?

'It's okay, dear. You don't have to thank me. That look on your face is more than enough.' Caroline smiled at her, and for the first time since they'd met Callie could see what it was about the woman that Blake cared about.

She returned Caroline's smile and walked back behind the screen, undressing slowly so that she didn't do any damage to the dress. When she was done, she handed it over to Caroline along with the shoes and the necklace.

'Caroline, I don't think I can take these from you.' She gestured to the accessories she knew must have cost a fortune.

'You can't have the dress if you don't.'

'What?'

Caroline put the dress in a clothing bag and said again, 'You can't wear this dress if you don't take the accessories.'

'Why...why not?'

'Because you need the whole package for Blake to get that feeling *you* had when you looked in the mirror.' Caroline smiled kindly when Callie lifted her eyebrows. 'You don't think I saw the surprise on your face when you looked at yourself? I think it would give Blake a good kick in the behind to see you like that. And, from what I know about that man, he could use it.'

Again, Callie didn't respond.

'I'm *so* glad he brought you here.'

Suddenly Callie found herself in Caroline's arms.

Hesitantly, she put her arms around the woman, and she felt an odd sense of comfort when she said, 'Be patient with him. He'll get there eventually.'

She drew back, and Caroline smiled again, and for a moment Callie wondered what 'there' meant. She realised too late that she'd asked Caroline out loud, and waited with bated breath for the answer.

'You'll know soon enough, dear,' she said, before calling Blake, and Callie knew her chance to probe was gone.

'Are you sorted?' Blake asked when he walked in.

'Yes, she is.' Caroline patted his cheek. 'No need for thanks. You can just send the things back after the event.'

'Of course. We can sort out payment at a later point.'

Callie immediately wanted to offer payment too—even though heaven only knew how she would be able to afford it—but Caroline had narrowed her eyes.

'Blake, you say something that offensive to me again, and I swear I will tell the world that you stole this dress from me.'

He laughed, and then sobered. 'I appreciate it, Caroline.'

'Anything for you.' For the first time, Caroline looked completely serious. 'I'm just so happy to see you, Blake. You look good.'

As they drove away Callie didn't say anything.

Caroline's cryptic words kept swirling around in her head, rousing the thoughts she had refused to have for such a long time. Rousing feelings she had ignored even when they had demanded attention. Because she couldn't give in to them. Not when she didn't know where she stood with Blake.

One moment she felt as if she didn't know this man she'd spent so much time with, the next he was kissing her as if he was a dying man and she was his last breath. And then he'd arranged this trip to a fairy godmother.

How could she love a man like that? she thought, and then went very still when she realised it.

The very simple truth that made his strange behaviour so difficult to swallow.

She looked away, out of the window, although she didn't see any of the buildings they passed. She just needed to look away from him. She didn't want him to know that she loved him. That she—Callie McKenzie, who hadn't thought she would ever open herself up enough to fall in love—was in love with her boss.

She squeezed her eyes closed, letting herself process the novelty of her thoughts.

Except that they weren't new, she thought. They had been there since—well, she didn't even know. But then Caroline had nudged her and cracked the armour she'd protected the thoughts in. She was in love with an incredible man. A man who cared about his company, about people, about *her*. A man who made her feel she wasn't alone. A man who had helped her work through feelings from the most difficult part of her past.

If she'd had to pick him from a list on paper, Callie would have put money on herself picking Blake, and a part of her took joy from that. But that joy was quickly dimmed by the fact that the man she had fallen in love with wasn't the man who was sitting next to her. And it terrified her—wholly and completely—to consider the reasons why that was the case.

She was so deep in thought that she didn't even notice that they'd stopped until Blake put a hand on her thigh.

'Callie?'

'Yeah?'

'We're here.'

She looked around in surprise. 'This isn't the hotel.'

'No, it isn't. This is the salon my stepmother goes to. I made an appointment for you, and a car will come and get you in a few hours.'

'Blake, this really isn't necessary...'

'A car will come and get you and bring you back in time for the event,' he repeated, and then he continued, 'There will probably be someone inside to help you with all the make-up stuff, too.'

'Blake—'

'No, don't say it. Don't tell me that you don't want this. Because this isn't about you. This is *for* you. You deserve this. After all you've done...' He lifted a hand to her face and she thought that it was as if he *needed* her to believe him. 'You deserve a few hours of relaxation. When people do things for *you*. Let me do this for you, okay?'

She wished she could just accept his words at face value. Her heart was full of him, of his compassion, of his gesture for her. But something told her that he'd said them out of obligation. Out of a need for her to accept this from him. And how could she resist such a plea?

'Okay.'

He leaned over and kissed her cheek. 'I'll see you in a little bit. Go and have fun.'

CHAPTER SIXTEEN

BLAKE WAS SURE he would burn a trail in the carpet if he didn't stop pacing.

But he felt unsettled and couldn't stop. Not when some of his employees passed him, smiling politely to hide their curiosity, or even when guests did, aiming puzzled looks at him as he walked back and forth in front of one of the rooms. He wasn't sure if it was adrenaline for what was to come during the evening that fuelled his legs, or anticipation at seeing Callie when she finally emerged from the room she was using to get ready in.

He hadn't seen her when she'd got back, so he didn't know what she had thought about the limo he had sent to pick her up. It might have been overkill, but he wanted her to feel like a princess tonight. He wanted her to know that the effort she had put into the hotel hadn't been for nothing. He wanted her to know that what they'd shared together *meant* something to him. Especially when he wouldn't be able to tell her himself...

He paused. He didn't want to think about those plans. He didn't want to think about the way he had put distance between them, about Callie's face every time he'd done so. He didn't want to think about leaving her when it was all too painful. When he was doing it because he couldn't bear to lose her, to disappoint her. He just wanted to spend one night with her without worrying about what it would do to them when he left. Or, worse, what it would do to her if he stayed and couldn't give her what she wanted.

But he wasn't running, he assured himself. He was just saving them both from the potential hurt.

But all thoughts froze in his head when she opened the door and hesitantly took two steps towards him.

The neckline of her gown lay lazily over her chest, hugging her curves and accelerating his heart. Especially when he saw a diamond necklace sparkling just above her breasts, as though it wanted to distract him and draw his attention to them at the same time. The rest of the dress was just as flattering, clinging to her curves and revealing legs that Blake now realised he had vastly under-appreciated. She wore silver shoes that wrapped around her legs from just below her knee, and never before had he found a pair of shoes more attractive.

Finally, when his body had settled, he rested his eyes on her face. Her hair was like silk, tied into some kind of intricate knot at the base of her skull. And her face was glowing, slightly red at his appraisal, and absolutely gorgeous.

'Hi...' she said huskily, and Blake had to check himself before he could speak.

'Hi. You look amazing.'

She smiled hesitantly, closed the door behind her, and Blake had the pleasure of seeing how much skin the back of the dress revealed. He wasn't sure which side of it he appreciated more, he thought, and smiled when she turned back to him. Just one night, he promised himself—and his conscience—and offered his arm.

'Thank you,' she said as she straightened the tiny train of the dress behind her.

When they got to the elevator he looked at her in question.

'It would probably be best if we took the elevator today,' she said, without moving.

He squeezed her hand. 'Don't worry, the electricity won't go off tonight. And if it does I've made sure the generator is working, so we won't get stuck.'

'Famous last words...' she breathed, and then straightened her shoulders and walked into the small box.

He smiled at her bravado, and selected the button for the rooftop. He knew she held her breath as they steadily moved up, and when the doors pinged open she let out a huge sigh of relief.

'You ready?' she asked, and turned to him, the tension of a few moments ago only slightly abated.

He refused to think about what the remainder of that tension meant.

'I think so.'

'Then let's do this.'

'Dance with me.'

Callie turned to Blake and had her refusal ready when she saw he had the same look on his face as that afternoon when he'd kissed her.

But he didn't wait for an answer. Instead he took her glass and placed it with his own on the closest waiter's tray. Then he led her to the dance floor and pulled her in close. Every nerve in her body was awakened and prickled with awareness at the feel of him against her. His hand pressed against her naked lower back and sent shivers down her spine, and when she looked up at him her breath caught.

He looked at her with longing, with a sadness she hadn't expected. But she didn't want to think about it. She didn't want to think about all that had plagued them over the last few days. No, tonight she wanted to stand in the middle of the dance floor on the rooftop, under the moonlight, and sway to the music with the man she loved.

'Callie?'

She lifted her head and the illusion of a few moments ago was gone. And it had taken any thoughts she had about love with it.

'What is it?'

He looked at her, his eyes filled with an emotion she knew only too well.

'We need to talk.'

She clenched her jaw as a voice in her head told

her that she wasn't being paranoid. She stiffened in his arms and looked at him, trying to read him even though it pained her to do so. And what she saw gave her the answer to all the questions she'd had.

'You're leaving.'

His arms tightened around her, and she had to stop herself from pulling away from him.

'Callie—'

'Don't.' She didn't look at him, and was grateful when the song ended. 'Just *don't*.'

She wanted to hate him for it—for doing this to her after making her feel like a princess. After making her fall in love with him. But she forced all feelings aside and worked the room, pretending everything was normal.

She clapped along with everybody else when Blake walked up onto the stage to thank everyone for coming, and laughed jovially when he told them he looked forward to taking their money the following week. But when the formalities were done she couldn't take it any more. She slipped away to Connor, and asked him if he could wrap things up for her.

'Yeah, sure. Things shouldn't go on too long

anyway.' He looked at her, and then frowned. 'Are you okay?'

'I'm fine.' She brushed a kiss over his cheek. 'Thanks. I've spoken to all the investors, so I know they're happy with the event. You just need to facilitate the clean-up afterwards. I'll see you soon, okay?'

She didn't wait for his response, though she could tell that his gaze was on her as she walked away from the event. She didn't look back as she took the stairs in her evening gown, too distressed to take a chance on the elevator. They had pulled it off, she thought, and immediately felt grief at the use of 'they' for her and Blake. There would be no more of that, she knew.

She laid a hand on the railing of the staircase, bracing herself for support, and took a moment—just one—to close her eyes and soothe her aching heart. But she knew that soothing wouldn't be possible—not when her pain could only be compared to what she'd felt after her parents had died. But still she stood, rubbing a hand over her chest, as though doing that would make a difference somehow.

The look on Blake's face flashed through her

eyes—the look that had told her all she needed to know about the awkwardness between them over the last few days—and another wave of grief rushed through her.

But instead of giving herself another moment, she hurried back to the room she had got ready in to change and get her things. Before she changed she looked in the mirror for one last time, wondering who the woman who looked back at her was. That woman looked so glamorous she might be royalty—nothing like the broken woman Callie knew really stood there. The one who was using every last bit of her strength to keep standing, not to fall into a heap on the floor and cry until she couldn't think about him any more.

Until she couldn't feel the pain that sliced through her at every memory of him.

She carefully took off the necklace and the shoes, placing them back into their boxes, and peeled the dress from her skin. When she was done she laid the dress bag over her arm and took the boxes in one hand, her own things in the other. She struggled out through the door and smiled her thanks when Tom, one of the bellboys, offered to help her.

She'd just handed over her things and asked him to call her a taxi when she heard Blake's voice.

'Callie—wait. Callie!' he said, more loudly when she didn't stop. 'I've been looking for you all over. We need to talk.'

She gestured for Tom to go ahead, and stiffened her spine when she saw Blake walking towards her even as the pain crushed through her chest.

'I'm on my way home. I was going to put this in your office with a note for Caroline. Actually, I think I'll do that now.'

She walked past him to his office, silently thanking Kate for getting her a room on the ground floor, so that she didn't have to get into an elevator again. She opened the door and laid the things gently over the desk Connor had put up for Blake, and turned when she heard the door slam.

'Let me explain,' he said, tension in every part of his body.

'Explain what?'

'Why I'm leaving.'

'So you *are* leaving.' She nodded as her heart broke, but coated it with anger. 'I thought you were just going to let me assume something was wrong, like you've been doing for the last few days.'

'I'm sorry. But—'

'I don't want to hear it, Blake.'

'Callie, I think the least you can do is let me explain myself.'

His tone was testy now, and she felt anger clutch at her.

'*Why*, Blake? Why should I let you explain yourself? You've been pushing me away for days. You've lied to me. And now you're leaving. So give me one reason why I shouldn't walk out of here right now and forget about whatever we had?'

'Because we care about each other. At least I care about you.' His hands were on his hips; his face was fierce. 'I care enough that I'm leaving because it's what's best for you.'

'What's *best* for me?' she repeated, almost shocked at his audacity. 'You've decided what's best for me based on what?'

'Based on the fact that I know you,' he said angrily. 'You need someone who can be a father to your children. I can't do that.'

Pieces began to fall into place somewhere at the back of her head, but she didn't take the time to see it. 'Of course you can't. Not when you're so stuck in your own world that you don't really care about how I feel.'

'Excuse me?'

Although she heard the warning in his voice, she couldn't stop now. 'I can't actually believe that I thought you might tell me what was going on in your head. I made excuses for you. I went against my gut.'

Tears pricked at her eyes, and for once she didn't care.

'That night you took me home from your house—the night you lied to me—I told myself that you needed time, and that I needed to be patient. But I waited and waited and waited. And all I got was distance, a day of pampering—because you needed to distract me from the fact that you were leaving, right? And from a decision made for my best interests. All because of what?'

She wiped at the tears that came when she realised that he had been saying goodbye to her from the day he'd dropped her at home. Today had just been the finale.

'Because you couldn't have a conversation with me about having a family?'

The shame she saw in his eyes confirmed her words.

'You have no idea what it's like to care about someone and realise that you can't give them what they want,' he said.

'*You* have no idea what it feels like to have someone you love decide they don't want to *give* you what you want,' she snapped back at him, and then stopped when the words fell between them like the blade on a guillotine.

'You *love* me?'

'I'll get over it—don't worry.'

It felt like a weakness, now—a mistake. Loving him. One she would rather have kept to herself. But she hadn't, and now she had to keep herself from falling for that expression on his face. It made her want to beg him to stay, to face his fears, to let himself love her.

To let her love be enough for him—for them.

But then she saw the sadness behind his surprise at her declaration—the sadness that told her he wouldn't let go of whatever was keeping them apart—and she felt devastation rip through her. With tears still threatening, she walked to the door, and then she paused, the fire inside her burning just enough for her to turn back to him.

'You could've missed it, because I made the mistake of saying I love you, so I'm going to say it again. You think that you're leaving because you can't give me what I want. But what I want is exactly what *you* want—a family. So don't use me as an excuse, Blake. The real problem here is *you*.'

'Callie…I'm trying. I mean, I've tried it before, and I failed miserably at being a father.' He said the words through clenched teeth. 'I'd rather walk away than have you witness me failing at it again.'

She choked back the sob that threatened, and felt completely helpless as she said, 'Well, then, luckily for both of us I'm used to the people I love leaving me.'

And with those words she walked out through the door, slamming it shut on him and on their relationship.

And breaking whatever had been left of her heart.

CHAPTER SEVENTEEN

BLAKE STOOD LOOKING OUT of the window of the office he shared with Connor, and felt the weight of his decision heavy on his shoulders. The weight that had settled there the moment Callie had shut the door to the office—to them— what felt like years ago.

He rubbed a hand over his face, tried to get his thoughts in order. The first day of negotiations had gone well—he thought he already knew who would be giving him a call, even though they still had four more days to go. It would take a few days after that to draw up the contracts, and then that would be the end of the personal responsibility he felt after letting the Elegance Hotel, Cape Town, slip through the cracks because of Julia.

He wouldn't be needed in Cape Town after that. He could run operations for the hotels from anywhere in the country. From anywhere in the *world*. Logically, he knew that. Which was why he couldn't figure out why every part of him wanted to stay in Cape Town.

Except that was a lie. He knew exactly why he wanted to stay. The part he couldn't figure out was how he could even consider it. He'd broken things off with Callie—whatever they'd had was now completely and utterly broken. His heart seemed to be, too—so much so that he couldn't remember the reasons he had given her, had convinced himself of, for why they couldn't be together. The reasons that had seemed so clear before.

'You should be at home, celebrating the deal that will be coming in soon.'

Blake turned to see Connor behind him, his hands in his pockets.

He nodded, failing to muster the energy required for a smile. 'I'm not in the mood.'

'I can see that. Seems you and Callie may have taken a drink from the same fountain. She's as miserable as you are.'

Blake hated it that there was a part of him that took comfort in that. 'She is?'

'Yes.' Connor waited a beat, and then said, 'In case you didn't pick it up, the fountain was a metaphor. The reality is that you two have been in a relationship that has now broken up. Correct?'

Blake stared at Connor, wondering why on earth his heart was thumping as though he had been caught making out with a girl by her parents, like some teenager. 'How did you find out?'

Connor let out a bark of laughter and Blake wondered if he had spoken with the guilt he felt.

'Blake, *you* may be able to hide your feelings quite well, but my sister can't.'

He smiled at that. 'Yes, so I've realised. She told you?'

'She didn't have to. I could see it from the way she looked at you.'

Connor studied Blake for some time, and Blake had to resist the urge to shuffle his feet. He was becoming increasingly aware of the fact that he was being sized up by his employee. No, he corrected himself. By the brother of the woman he cared about.

'Blake, do you know how long it took for me to get Callie to consider dating?' Connor shook his head. 'It was like talking to a rock. She would let me speak for however long my words of encouragement for that day required, and then she'd smile and tell me she wasn't interested. So, as much as I'd like to avoid getting involved in my boss's affairs, the fact that Callie opened up to you tells me that she cares about you. What happened?'

Blake felt another blow to his heart at Connor's words, and wondered why the reminder that Callie had been willing to let him in hurt so much.

'It doesn't matter. We can't be together.' He shrugged, as though to show that he had come to terms with it.

'Well, clearly it *does* matter—to both of you—because of exactly that.' He stopped, gave Blake a moment to contradict him, but when it didn't happen, he nodded. 'That's what I thought. Was it you or her?'

'What do you mean?'

'I mean did you end it or did she?'

Blake thought about it. 'I'm not actually sure. I suppose it was me—though she was the one who actually walked out.'

Connor stared at him, and then shook his head. 'Of course she would fall for you. You're *safe*.'

'Excuse me?'

'You're safe,' he repeated. 'You're not here permanently and you're her boss. She wouldn't have to worry about falling for you because you would never feel the same way about her.'

'That's not—'

'In fact she probably never told you how she really felt. She may not be able to hide her feelings, but verbalising them is completely different. So if you weren't looking, and she didn't say anything, you'd never know and she'd be able to tell herself that she tried and then move on.'

'Stop.'

The single word was said so sharply it might have sliced through metal.

'You have no idea what you're talking about. She put *everything* on the line for me.' Blake ran a hand through his hair. 'She told me exactly how she feels, and she was perfect. *I'm* the problem.'

Finally, after repeating the words had Callie told him the last time they'd spoken, something cleared inside his head. He *was* the problem. He had pushed her away because he'd thought that was best for them—for her.

He turned to Connor, saw the look on his face, and realised he'd been baited.

'How did you do it?' he asked Connor, who

was watching him with serious eyes. 'How did you get over your parents' deaths? In your relationship?' He saw the surprise on Connor's face and realised there was no point in pretending he didn't know. 'Callie told me you're expecting. Congratulations.'

'Thanks.' Connor paused, as though trying to gather his thoughts, and then he said, 'I'm sure you know that losing our parents broke both of us.' He rubbed at the back of his neck. 'When I found out Elizabeth was pregnant it scared me. I don't know how to be a father, and I was terrified of caring about her, about our baby, and then losing them. And then I realised that going through life being scared wasn't living. I thought about coming home to Elizabeth, to our child, and I realised my parents would have *wanted* that for me. They wanted me to live, to be happy.'

Blake thought about how he'd imagined the same thing, and how it had thrown him into a panic. 'And that was it?'

'Pretty much.' Connor shoved his hand back into his pocket. 'I'm still scared of losing them. I still don't know how I'll be a father. But the thought of not being with them, of *not* being a father, scares me more.'

Something shifted for Blake as he realised he felt the same way. The misery he felt now because he had lost her—the irony of that gave him a headache—was testament to that. But he still couldn't shake off that one thing...

'You had a father to learn from.'

'We all do. Even if they aren't perfect,' Connor continued when Blake opened his mouth to interrupt. 'We learn from them. We learn what to do and, sometimes more importantly, we learn what *not* to do. And we should have a partner to help us through it.' He smiled slightly. 'It's not so scary when you realise you're not alone. Unless, of course, you choose to be.'

He stopped, and then nodded at Blake.

'I think I'll head home now. And by the way...' Blake looked at Connor. 'I don't care if you're my boss. If you hurt her again I'll kick your butt.'

Blake smiled wanly in response, and then sat down heavily at his desk. Connor had a point. With Brent, Blake had tried to be there as much as possible, and he'd thought he had succeeded until the divorce. It was still a sore point for him, the fact that he couldn't be there for Brent now. One he had used when he'd decided he couldn't give Callie the family she needed.

She would be an amazing mother, he thought. She was caring—passionately so. And she would sacrifice her own happiness before letting anything happen to the people she cared about. He could only imagine what she'd do for her child, for her family. She would never leave them—not for one moment...

She would *never* leave, Blake realised. If Callie had any choice in the matter she wouldn't leave the people she loved. But *he* had left. He'd left her, failed her, disappointed her, lost her. All the things he'd wanted to protect her—and himself—from had happened, because he'd chosen to leave the woman he loved.

The realisation hit him like a bomb, and he leaned forward, bracing his arms on his knees. He loved her. And he had hurt her. So much so that the woman he knew in his heart would never leave the person she loved—*him*—had left. Because he had left her first. He'd done the very thing she'd been afraid of. He'd shown her that opening up to him had been a mistake.

Convincing her to take him back would mean she'd have to trust that he wouldn't leave again. And how could he do so when he'd already left?

The weight on his shoulders nearly crushed him.

Callie's heart broke over and over again each time she thought about it—which felt like every second of every day.

She had taken the week off work, which no one had questioned, despite the fact that she hadn't taken any time off since she'd started—because she couldn't bear to see Blake every day. Not when there was a hole in her chest where her heart was supposed to be.

She knew the pieces lay somewhere, broken in her chest, and would no doubt remind her of their brokenness when she saw him. She would forget, just for a second, about the fact that he had left her and she would run into his arms, feel his warmth, smell the comforting musk of his cologne.

And then she would break when she realised that would never happen again.

She shrugged her shoulders and forced herself

to breathe as she walked into the hotel on Friday. Kate had called, telling her that a young honeymooning couple had begged her to arrange a tour for them, and since Kate had no idea what to do she'd called Callie. Her favourite tours were those she organised for honeymooners—they were always so happy to be with one another it was infectious—so she'd reluctantly agreed to come in.

Even though she didn't want to see the man who'd broken her heart. The man who, according to her brother, was a negotiation tsar.

Of course she was happy that the negotiations were going well. But somehow it just didn't seem important any more. So she would just focus on what she'd come to do.

Kate had told her the couple wanted to see Table Mountain at sunset. That would be in an hour, giving her enough time to introduce herself and travel there with her guests. And to remember that the last time she had been up there had been with Blake.

She stopped when he materialised in front of her. And blinked just to make sure she wasn't imagining things. That she wasn't dreaming of him again.

'Callie.'

'Blake.'

She nodded, and hated it that her body heated at the memory of his. Even worse, that her heart still longed for him.

'I've missed you around here.'

'I've...er...' She cleared her throat. 'I've been on leave.'

'I know.' He put his hands in his pockets. 'I was hoping we could talk.'

'Yes, well...let's pretend you've left already, when there won't be any more talking between us,' she said, and then tried to walk past him.

But she stopped—as did her heart—when he placed a hand on her arm.

'Callie, please. I have to tell you something.'

She looked up at him, and though her heart urged her to agree her mind warned her not to. And for once she chose to listen.

'I think it would be best if we didn't speak any more.'

Their eyes locked for a moment, and then he let go of her arm.

'Okay.'

She nodded and walked away with an aching

heart and the sinking feeling that this might be the last time she spoke to her boss.

To the man she loved.

CHAPTER EIGHTEEN

'AND IF YOU look over there you'll see Camps Bay Beach and the Atlantic Ocean. Beautiful, isn't it?'

Callie pointed out the area for her guests, and watched the sun cast its orange glow over the city, grateful that Cape Town was showcasing its romance for the couple. She smiled and walked to the other side of the mountain, giving them privacy. And giving herself time to think, to grieve for the man she would have loved to share the experience of sunset on the mountain with.

'I don't think I've ever seen anything quite as beautiful in my life.'

Callie heard the words and for a brief moment wondered if she had conjured him up again. But when she turned around Blake was standing in front of her, looking directly at her.

She squared her shoulders. 'What are you doing here?'

'I came to talk. I thought that you would have no choice on a mountain.' He smiled slightly.

She bit her lip, feeling the heat of tears threaten. Why couldn't he just leave her be?

'How did you know I was here?'

'Kate. Connor. A number of other people who gladly offered me the information when they realised we were together.'

'You told them that?'

He took a step closer. 'I did. I wanted them to know how serious I am about the talk we're going to have.'

Her heart ached with longing, with heartbreak. The combination left her a little breathless.

'I have guests here, Blake' She gestured to the couple. 'I don't think I'll have much time to talk.'

'That's okay. They're with me.'

It took Callie a moment to process that. 'What do you mean, they're with you?' She repeated the words slowly, hoping it would help her make sense of it.

'I mean I asked some friends of mine to request a tour. I knew you wouldn't come if it wasn't for your guests, so I called in a favour.'

His eyes were so serious, so hopeful, that

her indignation faltered. And her heart wondered what was so important that he'd had to
pull strings to see her. She turned to the couple, who waved gaily at her, and felt the ends of
her mouth twitch. And then she noticed that the
mountain had cleared in the moments she'd spent
with Blake, and that her pretend guests were also
moving in the direction of the cable car.

'Blake, I think the last cable car of the day is
leaving.' She said the words even as her mind
told her that it wasn't supposed to happen for at
least another hour.

'No, there's one more. For us.'

She looked at him in surprise. 'How did you...?'
But she trailed off when she saw the determination and the slight desperation in his eyes. 'You
did all this for a moment alone with me?'

He nodded and took her hand. Tingles went up
her arm as he led her to the end of the mountain
where it overlooked the ocean. They stood there
like that for a while, and then he spoke.

'I've been trying to find the words to tell you
how sorry I am since the moment I realised how
wrong I was.' His hand tightened on hers, and
then he stuffed it in a pocket. 'I did things so

poorly. I made decisions for you, for us, without talking to you. I let my fears become more important than my need for you.'

He turned to her and she resisted the urge to comfort him.

'And I *do* need you—more than I've needed anything else in the world.'

Her lips trembled and she took a deep breath, trying to figure out what to say. But he continued before she had a chance to respond.

'I have been so miserable since you walked out through the door of that office. I justified my actions, and cursed them, and I went back and forth doing that for a long time. And then I spoke to Connor, and I knew I was wrong.'

'You *what*?'

Blake gave her a nervous smile. 'He caught me moping in the office and offered me some advice.' Then he grew serious. 'My whole life I've tried to avoid disappointing the people I care about. I thought that by being in control I could do that. And then you came along, and I've never felt less in control in my life.'

He exhaled, looked out to the ocean.

'I was falling for you even when I was trying

not to. Then we got to know one another, and I knew the falling would never stop. Not with you.'

He looked back at her and she felt her breath catch.

'It scared me, Callie. I've *never* felt the way I feel about you. And I began to think about how I'd lost my mother, how much it would break me if you left. I thought about Brent, about disappointing him, and how it would hurt if I did that to you. How I had failed in my marriage, with my family, and how I wouldn't survive if I failed *you*. If I failed to give you the family you deserved.'

He reached a hand up and touched her cheek, and without even realising it Callie leaned into it. 'I thought the only way to prevent that was to leave. I couldn't break you, disappoint you or fail you if I left. But by doing that I did *all* those things, and I'm so, *so* sorry.'

His voice broke and Callie took a step forward, wanting to comfort him.

'I know, Blake. I know that you thought you were doing the right thing.' She looked up at him, drew a ragged breath. 'I was scared, too. I realised I was in love with you but I had no commitment from you besides the things we'd shared.

I convinced myself that it was enough. I convinced myself that loving you would be okay even if I lost you. *Because* I loved you.'

She couldn't stop the tears now, even if she wanted to.

'And then I *did* lose you, and it hurt more than I could imagine because you *chose* to leave me.'

'I'm sorry.'

He pulled her into his arms, and the pieces of her heart stirred.

'For everything. I can't imagine ever hurting you like that again.' He drew back. 'I'm not going to leave, Callie. I will *never* leave you.'

'Why should I believe you?' She whispered the words that whirled around in her mind, keeping her from accepting what he was saying.

'Because this week has been the worst of my life.' He gently brushed a piece of hair from her face. 'And it's made me realise that I want to give you the family you want. I want to create a legacy with you.' He tipped her chin up so that she could look at him. 'Believe me, because I'm telling you I won't leave you. Trust me.'

'Why?'

'Because I love you, Callie. And if you still

love me let me prove to you for the rest of my life that I will stay with you. That I will fight for you. For *us*.'

And with those words—the words she'd dreamed about hearing from him—her broken heart healed and filled.

'I still love you.'

He smiled tenderly at her. 'I hoped you would.'

'So much that it scares me.'

She looked at him, and the agreement in his eyes comforted her.

'I am, too. So let's be scared together.'

He got down on one knee and Callie's heart pounded and melted at the same time. Suddenly she became aware that the sun had set and that their only source of light now came from candles and lanterns, all over the top of the mountain. And then she saw the ring—a large diamond sparkling brightly up at her surrounded by what seemed like a thousand smaller ones—and she realised Blake was offering her the biggest assurance he could that he was staying.

'Will you marry me, Callie McKenzie?'

'You want to *marry* me?'

'I really, really do.'

She laughed, and nodded, and was swept up into his arms before she had a chance to wipe the tears from her cheeks. Her hand shook as he slid the ring on her finger, and then he kissed her, and any remnants of fear she'd had disappeared. The kiss was filled with all the longing they'd felt for one another since they'd been apart, with the joy of their future together, with the heat of their passion. And when they finally drew apart they were both breathing heavily.

'We're engaged,' she said when she'd recovered, and she looked at the ring on her finger.

'We are.' He smiled and drew her back against him. 'I'm thinking we should get married at the hotel. A rooftop sunset wedding could be pretty amazing.'

'I think that would be perfect.' And then she realised she hadn't even asked him about the deal. 'Did we get an investor?'

'We did. Marco signed the papers a few hours ago. He's going to be a silent investor. Although he *did* say he will still actively try to poach you.' He waited as she laughed, and then said, 'I have so many plans for the hotels. I can't wait to do it all with you.'

'So I'm going to help with the Owen legacy, huh?' She smiled and drew his hands tighter around her waist as they looked down at Cape Town at night.

'Yeah. Which means it's probably only fair that I help you with *your* legacy.' He looked down at her with a glint of amusement in his eyes. 'Family, right? I think the best way for me to show my commitment to you is if we start on that as soon as possible.'

Her laughter rang out on the top of Table Mountain, and for the first time since her parents had died Callie finally felt whole.

EPILOGUE

'ARE YOU READY for that?'

Blake gestured towards the chubby toddler who was steadily making his way over the grass in their backyard to his father, knocking down every toy they'd put out for him. He gave a happy gurgle when Connor picked him up and spun him around, and Callie smiled when she saw the absolute love in her brother's eyes as he did so.

'I keep thinking about a little girl with your eyes, or a boy with your hair. And every time I do I fall in love with the little person in my imagination.' Callie snuggled closer to her husband—she would never tire of the thrill that went through her when she thought that Blake was her *husband*—and kicked at the ground so that the swing seat they were sitting on would move.

She couldn't quite believe they were already celebrating her nephew's first birthday. Tyler was such a little ball of happiness, with his father's steady presence and his mother's zest for life, that it made her excited to see what combination her own child would be.

She resisted the urge to rub her stomach and imagined how happy her parents would have been if they'd been there. They would have loved enjoying their grandson in their home—the home that she and Blake now shared and had gladly offered to host Tyler's birthday at—and feeling the comfort of family. Connor and Elizabeth hadn't wanted a big party for their son when he wouldn't remember it, so instead they'd just organised a day when the McKenzies and the Owens—she *and* her brother had married within a few months of each other—could spend time together.

Callie couldn't think of a more perfect way to celebrate. Or to share her very exciting news.

'What if they have *your* eyes or hair?' Blake said, distracting her from her thoughts.

He pulled her in and she felt the warmth right down to her toes, before it quickly turned into a sizzle the moment he began to run his fingers up and down her bare arm.

'I suppose we'll have to accept them as they

are. It won't be *their* fault after all.' She gave a dramatic sigh, and smiled when Blake laughed.

She loved seeing him like this—relaxed, happy, content. He had become a part of their family so smoothly she sometimes felt that he had always been a part of it. And she wondered where the man who had feared family so much had disappeared to.

'Look how beautiful it is,' Blake said, and gestured to the mountain and the ocean they could see from the swing seat. She smiled when she saw the peace settle over him, the way it always did when he looked out onto that view.

'Are *you* ready for it?' she asked quietly, not wanting to be overheard by her brother and sister-in-law.

'What?' He followed her eyes with his as she looked at her nephew, and then settled them back on her. 'I was ready the moment I met you. And then again when you told me you'd marry me. I believe I was willing to start right at that moment.'

She laughed. 'You were. But there were a few things we needed to sort out first.'

He rolled his eyes—a clear indication of a man

who had heard the words before. 'Yes, I know. We had to set up our operations for the hotels from Cape Town, and then we had to support Connor and Elizabeth during their wedding and Tyler's birth, and then we had our own wedding.'

'Exactly. Points to you for remembering.' She grinned at the amusement in his eyes, and then felt it soften to a smile. 'But all that's done now.'

'Yes—thankfully. So I don't have to be reminded about it all the time.'

She felt her lips twitch. 'No, Blake, all that's done now.'

'I heard you the first time.' Blake frowned at her, and then sat up a little straighter. 'You mean we can start trying for a family?'

'I mean that it's happened without us really trying.' She whispered the words, unsure, even though she knew that this was what they both wanted. 'I think my body knew about our timeline, too.'

He took a moment to process her words, and then whispered back, 'Do you think you're pregnant?'

'I *know* I am. The doctor called yesterday.'

* * *

She had barely finished saying the words before Blake pulled her into his arms, needing the contact with her more than he'd thought possible. His heart was exploding, and it was a long time before he let Callie go.

'Hey, none of that in front of my kid.'

Blake heard Connor's amusement and smiled, unable even to pretend that he was upset. 'Well, I think expressions of love are important. Maybe we should start making notes of all the things we've learnt from Connor about what to do and what not to do before *our* baby gets here, honey.'

Connor's eyes widened. 'You're *pregnant*?'

Blake laughed, and thought he had never felt this good in his life. 'No, not me personally—but Callie is.'

The announcement was met with laughter and congratulations, and even though he accepted the hugs of his family, even though he toasted his unborn child, he couldn't take his eyes off Callie. She was radiant, he thought, and saw her blushing every time she caught him looking at her.

It made him love her even more.

When Connor and Elizabeth had left, Callie

and Blake moved back to the swing seat in the backyard. It would be a special place to him for ever, he thought. This house where he had finally found a home, where he had finally found himself be a part of a family. This yard where he had celebrated his godson's first birthday. And now this swing seat, where he had found out he was going to be a father.

'How have you made every dream of mine come true?' he asked, his heart filled with the love that overwhelmed him every time he looked at her.

She gave him that soft smile of hers and moved closer to him. 'We've made each other's dreams come true.' She laid a hand on his cheek. 'You're going to make the best father, Blake Owen.'

'Our child will have the best parents in the world.'

And then he kissed her, and knew without a doubt that he had finally found his home.

If you enjoyed Therese's debut book, and want to indulge with more working-together romances, make sure you try the magical Christmas quartet,
MAIDS UNDER THE MISTLETOE!

A COUNTESS FOR CHRISTMAS
by Christy McKellen
GREEK TYCOON'S MISTLETOE PROPOSAL
by Kandy Shepherd
CHRISTMAS IN THE BOSS'S CASTLE
by Scarlet Wilson
HER NEW YEAR BABY SECRET
by Jessica Gilmore

MILLS & BOON®
Large Print – May 2017

A Deal for the Di Sione Ring
Jennifer Hayward

The Italian's Pregnant Virgin
Maisey Yates

A Dangerous Taste of Passion
Anne Mather

Bought to Carry His Heir
Jane Porter

Married for the Greek's Convenience
Michelle Smart

Bound by His Desert Diamond
Andie Brock

A Child Claimed by Gold
Rachael Thomas

Her New Year Baby Secret
Jessica Gilmore

Slow Dance with the Best Man
Sophie Pembroke

The Prince's Convenient Proposal
Barbara Hannay

The Tycoon's Reluctant Cinderella
Therese Beharrie

MILLS & BOON®
Large Print – June 2017

The Last Di Sione Claims His Prize
Maisey Yates

Bought to Wear the Billionaire's Ring
Cathy Williams

The Desert King's Blackmailed Bride
Lynne Graham

Bride by Royal Decree
Caitlin Crews

The Consequence of His Vengeance
Jennie Lucas

The Sheikh's Secret Son
Maggie Cox

Acquired by Her Greek Boss
Chantelle Shaw

The Sheikh's Convenient Princess
Liz Fielding

The Unforgettable Spanish Tycoon
Christy McKellen

The Billionaire of Coral Bay
Nikki Logan

Her First-Date Honeymoon
Katrina Cudmore

0517 Rom LP